The Coalition

Myra Miller

PublishAmerica
Baltimore

© 2006 by Myra Miller.
All rights reserved. No part of this book may be reproduced, stored in a retrieval system or transmitted in any form or by any means without the prior written permission of the publishers, except by a reviewer who may quote brief passages in a review to be printed in a newspaper, magazine or journal.

First printing

All characters appearing in this work are fictitious. Any resemblance to real persons, living or dead, is purely coincidental.

At the specific preference of the author, PublishAmerica allowed this work to remain exactly as the author intended, verbatim, without editorial input.

ISBN: 1-4241-1391-1
PUBLISHED BY PUBLISHAMERICA, LLLP
www.publishamerica.com
Baltimore

Printed in the United States of America

To my husband, Sal, for love and support; to Steve Leatherwood, the best manager B. Dalton will ever have, for encouragement and writing support; to Valerie Schmale for endless readings and edits; to my family for missed hours and understanding why; and to all those persons who granted me permission for the use of their real names, family names, nicknames, and near names—I love you all.

Prologue

December 12, 2014
State Capitol Building
Harrisburg, Pennsylvania

It was evening at the Pennsylvania State House and Frances Haynes had just finished dusting one wall of objects in the East Wing of the Welcome Center. As she pushed her cleaning cart across the marble-floored atrium she approached the Welcome Desk where the night guard, Rob Porter, sat monitoring a bank of security cameras.

Her image was still visible on one screen as Rob looked up and greeted her. "Evening Ms. Francis. Not too many marks today, I hope."

Slowing her steps, she smiled and replied, "Oh, just the normal smears here and there where people can't seem to resist a touch or two. But, after twenty-two years on the job I can spot a smudge ten yards away." Once cleared of the desk area she called back over her shoulder, "Have a quiet evening Rob and I'll see you on my way out. Bye. Bye."

Continuing on, she dusted and cleaned a few founding father busts, having quiet personal conversations with each figure. When dusting The Founding Father, she commented, "Shame on you, Mr. Penn, you're a mess! One of these days I'll have to knit you a little cap to keep the dust off."

That chore completed, she started her routine of tidying up the public visitors rooms. The room that holds public deeds and grants was always her first choice, as this was always the messiest. People loved to pour through the files and left the papers wherever they had finished reading them. She gathered the papers and made a neat stack at the end of the long conference room sized reading table. In the morning state office workers would re-file the papers.

Tonight, as she entered the room, she noticed that one visitor had over stayed the hours. A man seated at the reading table had fallen asleep over a pile of papers. This was not unheard of, just against the rules. Well, nothing to do but wake him up and show him the door. As she nudged him to wake him up, he slipped out of the chair, his glassy eyes staring at the ceiling. Even from the football field distance to the security station down the hall, Rob heard her echoing screams.

Rob entered the room with his gun drawn. Following the line of vision where Frances was staring, he took a deep breath to steady himself and holstered the weapon. The man on the floor did not appear to pose a threat. In an attempt to convey sympathy, as he neared Frances, he touched her shoulder from behind. Unaware that anyone had entered the room, this gesture had her screaming louder, if possible, and jumping away from his hand. This movement brought her foot into contact with the body on the floor. Yep, she could yell louder.

Rob moved in front of her so she would see him. She stopped in mid-scream and pointed. Rob nodded his understanding as he bent over the body searching for a pulse. None. He looked around the body for signs of blood. None. He even scanned the body for any signs of trauma. None. Straightening up, he placed an arm around Frances' shoulders, turned her away from the body and towards the door. He talked to her as he guided her out of the room, "It's alright, Ms. Frances. Don't worry, I'm here. Everything is going to be okay. Calm down now, I'll take care of everything."

He slowly got her shaking form down the hall to the security station. "You sit down right here in my chair. You had one good scare back there. I'm going to call the police and contact the guys that are working in other spots around the building." Frances looked at him with glazed eyes, jumped out of the chair and grabbed his arm with both of her hands. Extracting his arm from her grip, he eased her back into the chair. "Don't worry Ms. Frances, I'm not going anywhere. I'm not going to leave you alone."

He made the calls from the desk phone next to her chair. "Do you want me to call your husband for you...maybe have him come to get you?" Frances nodded yes. Rob also called the housekeeping supervisor on duty.

Within thirty minutes the Welcome Center looked like a practice session for an upcoming inauguration day. Everyone was there; State Police, County Police, Harrisburg Police, Homeland Security, and Capitol Security. The county coroner's office had been notified and was on the way. Crime Scene Investigators (CSI) had already taped off the reading room and were doing their scientific magic to retrieve clues.

All the maintenance personnel were gathered in the atrium entrance area where they were questioned by the State Police. They were questioned about seeing anything unusual or suspicious during their shift. Then they were escorted to their lockers to get their personal effects and released for the evening. Frances was the first questioned and then released into her husband's care.

One Capitol policeman returned from searching the lower level of the building eager to speak with his superior. "Boss, you're not going to like this, but there's another body downstairs."

The second body was discovered in the men's shower room of the cipher-locked exercise room. This is a self-regulated exercise room for the employees. They keyed themselves in, provided their own padlocks for their lockers, and signed up for the time usage on the equipment. A quick dusting and finger printing of the body by the CSI would show this man's prints matched some prints on the gym entrance.

As the lead CSI entered the wash area he spoke to no one in particular and to any one in ear shot, "So, who do we have here? It would seem he was a state employee, being in the employees' gym."

The second John Doe was on the tile floor in the men's room. He was lying at the base of a sink that was dripping an overflow stream from the sink onto his exercise shoes. Again, no pulse. Again, no blood. Again, no signs of trauma. Again, no outward explanation for death.

Security Guard Rob had opened the gym for the police and stood watch to keep the scene as undisturbed as possible. Internally he mused; Was this it? Just the two bodies? Were there more anywhere else in the building? What happened to them? Something they ate? Maybe from a machine here? Maybe from a machine he personally used for snacks? Was it something in the air? Something he was breathing right now?

Oh, Lord, he thought, this had to be the worst day he ever had on the job. In fact, he definitely would call this one a killer of a day.

CHAPTER I

Christmas Eve, 2014
Custis-Lee Mansion, Arlington, VA

    A request to attend the Christmas Eve gala at the historic Custis-Lee Mansion was a much sought after and coveted invitation. The guest list read like a "Who's Who" of political, financial and celebrated fame. Long considered the elite core of individuals holding substantial influence within the power base of Washington, DC.
    The building, a majestic four story mansion, was the seat of family life for such distinguished occupants as Washington, Custis, and Lee. Christmas Eve at the Mansion was a step back in time. The top floor had been renovated to the ballroom Robert E. Lee envisioned nearly two hundred years ago. Marble fireplaces are positioned at either end of the room and were draped in the holiday theme of boughs and holly. The chandeliers housed electric lights resembling flickering flames that maintained the grandeur of Antebellum Virginia.
    Entering the ballroom, guests were treated to the perfect holiday party of every childhood dream. It was a virtual feast of sight, scent and sound. Cherrywood furniture shone from dedicated polishing. Reflecting the light in the room, silver glistened and crystal sparkled. The air was perfumed with holiday fragrances of winter pine, cinnamon and berries. Banquet tables abounded with all manners of foods emitting delectable aromas of baked goods and roasted meats. Positioned in one corner of the room was an eight-piece stringed orchestra. They provided background music that favored seasonal carols and hymns. The annual festivity began in 1955 when the mansion was declared a permanent memorial. Over the years it became an

expected protocol to have the senior ranking senator host the prestigious event. For the past three years, that host has been the senator from New Jersey, J. T. Cerio.

At sixty-three J.T. had been a member of Congress for thirty-two years; first as a Representative, and now a four term Senator. Stationed at the head of the receiving line with his wife and the two youngest of their four sons, J. T. exhibited the charisma for which he was renowned. He hoped his performance carried off the expected holiday atmosphere as he shook hands, smiled, and engaged in small talk with each guest.

As well as those Congressional members in attendance, the guests included many famous, and nearly famous, dignitaries. Most prominent of the local populace was the new, first term Mayor, Yale Jackson. He and his wife were next in the receiving line. In addition to this being Yale's first major Christmas function in his elected position; it was his first ever visit to the Custis-Lee Museum. As he observed all the trapping such an establishment collected over the centuries and that were now on display, he recognized the signs that he was both impressed by and overwhelmed by the experience; he was sweating and had the sense that someone had just sucker-punched him. As he reached the head of the line, he took the host's hand firmly between both of his and exuded his best political smile. He felt the sweat in his armpits increase as he expressed his honor at being able to represent the District on such a prestigious occasion.

Quickly, maybe too quickly, he extended his wishes for a pleasant and peaceful holiday for the host and his family. Realizing that he was not putting his best foot forward, he felt it would be better to make the greeting short and the exit swift. He managed the departing obligatory handshake without the host needing to wipe Yale's sweat from his palms. In a further display of nervousness, he placed his hand in the small of his wife's back and nudged her away from the receiving line. Yale saw himself as small fry in this pond of giant trout. Yale knew his nervousness would be calmed with a small glass of White Zinfindel, a remedy he was now going after.

Trailing behind the Mayor in line was the very outspoken, colorful, Chairman of the Coalition for District of Columbia Statehood, Richard

Von Mumser, and his wife, Sandra. He, personally, enjoyed being called "The Local Boy" because that was exactly how he saw himself. At fifty-eight, Richard had been the self-proclaimed crusader of DC statehood for the past decade. His deceased father, a former District Mayor, harbored great personal disappointment that statehood was the only campaign pledge he was not able to fulfill.

Richard, a tenth generation Von Mumser, has local roots traceable back to the district foundation in 1790. Family legend has it that one of his ancestors was a member of the Ellicott and Banneker survey team that established the original boundaries for the then named Territory of Columbia. His ancestors were regular visitors at this estate since the laying of the original foundation.

As Richard and Sandra approached the Cerios, J.T. enthusiastically reached for Richard's hand as he remarked, "Richard, I am so glad that you, of all the guests, were able to be here tonight. Your presence here serves as a symbol of continuance, knowing that your family has almost as much history with this mansion as the namesakes."

At six feet two inches, and ramrod straight, Richard stood a good five inches taller than Cerio. Bending forward, he grasped J.T.'s outstretched hand in a hearty warm grip. "Yes, Senator, I agree. I am proud to say that every visit by a Von Mumser to local historical sites, such as this elegant building, only reaffirms my family's endurance as native Washingtonians. Statehood or not, we are still here while much more prominent families have crested and faded away."

Not one to ever pass up an opportunity to foot stomp for his dedicated mission, he continued, "You, yourself, come from one of the first liberated colonies. I am sure you understand the value and importance of self rule and statehood."

"As you know, I was in Trenton last week visiting with Governor Demasi. I know that I am repeating what I told him, but your support for the upcoming legislation on D.C. statehood would go a long way with other Congressional committee members."

Standing at an angle to the receiving line, slightly behind Senator Cerio, was Julius Walsh, a featured writer for the *DC Daily News*, recording the guests for possible inserts in tomorrow's Christmas

Edition. Sensing Von Mumser about to go "soap box" on the host, Julius called out to him, "Mr. Chairman....Richard, I see you believe in no rest for the weary when it involves the statehood issue. How goes the efforts? Anything new you want to share with the District residents?"

More persuasively adding, "Sort of like a Christmas present for the citizens? I could see it gets into tomorrow's edition."

Richard sheepishly looked at J.T. and offered his apologies for the political tactics, but not for the content of the words. Lifting the left side of his mouth, in a conspiratorial smile, J. T. patted Richard on the shoulder. "No apologies are necessary. I certainly understand and respect conviction. I promise to consider your issue."

Shaking J.T.'s hand in acknowledgement that the chitchat was over; Richard turned back to the reporter, "Julius, my man, you are fortunate indeed. I have developed a new platform strategy. What say we move to a less noisy spot while I explain to you the basic needs that drove the original colonies to push-the-envelop for statehood?"

"Sure, Sir, that would be great. Just a minute while I find a replacement to stand my place by the Senator. You just never know if the President or the Vice-President will show up and they always make for good news and great sales."

Julius was a reporter with a consuming desire to be The Reporter at the right place when a historic event happens, like the confirmation of DC statehood. He had been following the Chairman's efforts for the past several years. So much so, that inside the editorial department of the *Daily News*, he was referred to as Richard's Press Secretary. Julius got another Daily reporter to take over his position and followed the Chairman to another room on a lower level.

In Julius' absence, the stand-in reporter was the one to record the handshake and exchange of condolences between J.T. Cerio and the Senator from Pennsylvania, Greg Castello. Due to the strangest of circumstances, Pennsylvania, like New Jersey, recently had strange deaths occur at its state capitol building. About two-weeks ago, two male bodies were found in the building by the night shift personnel. Besides being bordering states, the two congressmen formed a working relationship that supported each other's legislative efforts when it was beneficial to the states' citizens.

Castello opened the conversation, "Hello, J.T., how goes it? I don't see your big boys tonight. Don't tell me they are finally tired of all the political merry making."

Smiling at his friend, J. T. explained, "No, the two older boys, and their wives, are back home in Trenton, devoting their holiday time with the family members of the three men who mysteriously died last week at the state capitol building. Governor Demasi arranged a special midnight memorial service for the three families. The intention is for the families to know that their joint grief is felt and shared by all the people of New Jersey."

Cerio was a man with strong family values that sometimes conflicted with his equally deep-rooted sense of public service on behalf of the residents of New Jersey. This annual event was an example of just such a struggle; needing to stand well for his constituents by staying for this appearance in Washington, and needing to stand with his constituents at the memorial in Trenton. The pride he knows as a father increased when his sons volunteered…no, demanded, to go home and represent their family, as the situation dictated.

Greg nodded his head in understanding, "I am so sorry that both of our states had to experience these unexpected and, as yet, unexplained deaths. As far as I have been told, these men had nothing in common, other than visiting the state buildings. You don't think that it has anything to do with the cleansing chemicals we use, do you? I'm making a mental note here to check to see if we use the same contract firms, or at the least, the same cleaning products. This way I will feel as if I am doing something."

J.T. replied, "That is a good idea. I am going to let the Governor know that someone will be calling the state employment office in Trenton and that they should be supportive of your efforts. Let us pray that this is just one of those truly bizarre situations and that no one else is going to be stricken."

"Amen to that Cerio. Amen to that thought."

CHAPTER II

January 3, 2015
Captions in *USA Today*
State-by-State Column:

GEORGIA: In Atlanta, four bodies found in the State Capitol Building yesterday. Names being withheld pending notification of next of kin. No immediate cause known for the deaths, remain a mystery. State police still investigating scene for clues.

NEW JERSEY: Three deaths from Dec 18th remain a mystery. No cause for sudden deaths available at this time.

PENNSYLVANIA: Two deaths from Dec 10th remain a mystery. No cause for sudden deaths available at this time.

CHAPTER III

January 3, 2015
Governor's Mansion
Atlanta, Georgia

Responding to a call from Governor Rory Froehlich, Atlanta's Chief of Police, Hank Sager, entered the working office at the Governor's mansion. Every time Hank entered this room he was struck a new at its pretentious design attempts to resemble a supreme British legal chamber.

Hank had a sense of being admitted to some majestic inner sanctum. His heavy duty steel toed work shoes made no sound as he crossed the open area from the double doors to the eighteenth century writing desk positioned in front of the floor to ceiling windows at the far side of the room. This massive area vibrated with the elegance so fabled of Southern plantations.

In the center of the seventeen foot high ceiling, a grand chandelier hung, supported by thin wires anchored in the floor above. This elegant fixture featured heavy teardrop crystals at the base of each globe shaped light bulb.

To the right side of the entry were built-in floor to ceiling bookcases. There was a sliding stepladder attached to a lip along the top shelf. From their precisely aligned pristine spines Hank would lay odds that those books had never been opened. He felt this was for special effects.

The left wall housed a fireplace large enough for a six foot man to stand in. The fireplace was defined by a two foot wide imported Italian marble ledge and matching marble sides. The obligatory ancestral oils hung above and to the sides of the fireplace. Semicircle to the fireplace was a seating area with Moroccan leather winged back chairs, each having its own mahogany end table holding a reading lamp with room for a drink coaster and small pastries.

Mahogany sideboards lined the walls on either side of the double doors. Central on each table was a fresh cut flower arrangement artistically displayed in an overblown cut glass bowl and surrounded by small brass, pewter, and Dresden china family heirlooms.

The windowed far side of the room overlooked a rolling expanse of lawn that would reflect emerald green in season. A few feet into the room's depth from the windows was the Governor's working area. The over sized Dufief antique desk was flanked in front with four more Moroccan leather chairs. Positioned a few feet to one side was a fully stocked drink caddy. A fax machine and laptop computer occupied a wooden tray style serving trolley on the other side.

As he neared the Governor, Hank had two thoughts: this area must have been a ballroom at some point in its history and if this museum environment was how the top layer of society lived, he was glad his world was farther down the ladder—closer to his favorite take out shop and drinking hole. That latter thought had a smile lurking at his mouth.

Governor Froehlich looked up at just that moment and frowned. "Just what do you find so amusing? We have four…count them, one…two…three…four unexplained dead bodies that were living, breathing human beings yesterday. Is that what you find so damn funny? Because I sure as hell don't find anything humorous here."

Before Sager could reply, Froehlich rose from his seat behind the desk and walked out in front to face the Chief. Hank noticed that the usually spry, energetic sixty-five year old man looked as if he had been up all night. His blue eyes were bloodshot, his immaculately styled salt and pepper hair appeared finger combed and his navy blue Brooks Brothers suit had far too many creases for a morning's wear.

"Look Hank, I know we have our own history that might not exactly stand up to a close inspection, but these deaths have really gotten to me. I mean, here we are, and rallying up as the statistics show our crime rate going down. And then, BAM! without warning, four unexpected and unexplained deaths. Right here! In the state capitol building of all places. **And**, in an election year to boot. Where were all the security people? Didn't anyone see anything? There must have been hundreds of people in the visitors' area yesterday. What-a hell of a way to start a new rating period. Don't get me wrong, I am sorry for the family members. I understand the men were all native Georgians...No out of state tourists. I guess that is one good thing."

Hank, being familiar with the Governor's tirades, lets his thoughts drift as he recounted his association with Froehlich.

At thirty-nine, Hank was the youngest Chief of Police in Atlanta's history. He joined the police force right out of high school. While not technically overweight, he was definitely a larger-than-life individual. He stands six feet three inches and weights in at approximately two hundred and seventy pounds. He proudly displays his full head of thick, wavy, reddish brown hair worn in a typical military short haircut. The Chief's oval face was quite memorable partly due to the pockmarks remaining from his childhood bout with measles, and partly due to the very piercing appearance of his almost transparent light blue eyes. Suspects have been known to rapidly provide confessions when left to face him alone. By looks alone, Hank's stare had intimidated many a suspect to confess to those crimes for which they were being questioned and even to other previously unknown crimes; all in the hopes of escaping the Chief's presence. Hank was quite proud of his conviction rate.

Ten years ago, he came into the radar of Governor Froehlich. It was during an election campaign when an irate constituent came into the assembly room, took his place at the end of the greeting line, nervously shifting his weight from one foot to the other. He spoke loudly to all within the room, accusing the Governor of procrastinating on the No-Tolerance-Rule on school property legislation. He said that this delay in passage caused his daughter to have been caught in the cross hairs of a schoolyard shooting that left her wheel chair dependent for the rest of her life. This distraught father then jumped the line, walked straight to the head position and got nose-to-nose with Governor Froehlich, booming insults as loud as his lungs would allow, his face getting a ruddy glow and pure hate pouring from his eyes.

Sensing pending violence, then Patrolman Sager interceded by stepping behind the intruder and physically restraining the man in a two armed lock around the middle that pinned his arms in place. The man seemed to snap out of his diatribe at this point and broke into sobs about both his actions and his daughter's condition. The Governor, ever conscience of public appearances, expressed his sorrow about the girl's situation, refused to press charges, and promised a speedy review of the pending legislation. The father was humbled by the Governor's display of sympathy and accepted Froehlich's outstretched hand, offered as a gesture of compassion. The man thanked the Governor and continued to call out his gratitude and apologies as the security guards led him away.

That encounter led to swift promotions through the ranks for Hank. Within an amazingly short span of five years, Hank found himself the Chief of Police. At the same time, by an unspoken understanding, Hank Sager became the Governor's "man". It was Hank that the Governor would call to quietly make unpleasant issues disappear.

Froehlich's rising tone of irritation brought Hank back to the present.

"I suppose another blessing is that no one from that visiting DC group was involved. That would just have made this issue perfect—to have a visiting dignitary, or one of his aides, meet their end while visiting here.

That reminds me, I promised that Von Mumser guy I would talk with Senator Lukavec about that statehood issue. I, personally, wouldn't bet on it doing any good…but, a promise is a promise."

At that comment, Hank thought; "*Yeah, sure, honor among thieves.*"

The Governor was finally getting down to the reason that he summoned Hank to the mansion. "I want this situation looked into immediately and solved even sooner. This is no way to boast that the crime rate in Atlanta is decreasing with four unexpected and unsolved deaths literally on our doorstep. I don't care how many people you have to put on the case. I want to know the causes of death.

And, if it is not natural causes, I want to know what the cause was and who is the most likely person that would have committed the crime. Got that, Chief? And for pity's sake, don't even try to connect this with those deaths up north in that damn Yankee State of New

Jersey, okay? Whatever happens here needs to stay here. We take care of our own issues."

From his long association with Froehlich, Sager knew better than to point out that other law enforcement agencies were already on the scene, and there was talk about bringing the Center for Disease Control in for an added look at possible foul play. He also recognized that this was the best time to leave. Taking a deep breath to indicate submission to the Governor's direction, Hank departed with, "Yes, Sir. I'll get my best men on this ASAP. You'll have daily updates, and more, if anything new develops."

CHAPTER IV

January 3, 2015
Chief Editor's Office
DC Daily News Building
Washington, DC

Chief Editor, Don Wellen, was a lie to the stereotype portly, brow beating, bellowing newspaper man-in-charge. At fifty-eight, Wellen maintained a lean five feet ten inch frame through a devout exercise regime and a low fat diet. The hair may tend to the gray side, but the body was as good as any thirty-five year old. Today was one of those rare occasions when he was truly riled. He felt frustrated enough to punch someone.

Not just anyone, there was definitely a certain someone, Julius Walsh, his "Ace" reporter. Don thought that if this were the *Daily Planet*, then he would be *Perry White*, and Julius would surely be his *Jimmy Olsen*; always eager, generally off track. Well, seems *Jimmy* was staying true to form, not seeing the forest for the trees.

Pacing back and forth in his empty office, Wellen resorted to an age old habit, muttering to himself when aggravated, "Damn, we had a guy on the scene in Atlanta yesterday. Why didn't Julius send us something to put in our paper? Those guys across the river in Virginia at the *USA Today* building seem to have the inside scoop on all the juicy articles."

Wellen decided it would be easier on his stress level to share his thoughts with the reporter in question. As he dialed Julius' cell number, he was determined that it was time for Julius and him to have a talk about what's hot and what's not—for the interest of the DC readers. Walsh had been a boil on the butt of the "Chairman", Julius' nickname for Chairman Richard Von Mumser, long enough. There were only so many ways that Von Mumser could campaign, politic, or schmooze the Governors and Congressmen for support of a referendum on statehood. Yes, Mr. Walsh needed to sever this need to cover the historical trail documentary and get back here where he could cover **real** items of interest for the populace of DC.

Hearing Julius' voice, the Editor cuts off the greetings, "Mr. Walsh, this is Mr. Wellen...Your Boss. Remember me?"

"Hi, Boss! Wow, you're calling about my transmission already? It seems that I just pushed the send button. Great pictures, huh?"

"Kid, I have no idea what you're babbling on about. The reason for this call is to tell you to come back here. Enough history hunting. I need you here, in DC."

Julius tried to get the Editor's attention, "But, Boss..." Wellen was not going to be stopped.

"Besides, you have been like a second skin on Von Mumser. You have shadowed his every move for several years. This includes all those out of town trips he takes. And now, on the last two trips, you were right on location where people mysteriously kicked the bucket. Did you cover the story for us? No! Did you even interview the local authorities to get their spin? No! So, how do you think I know there was mayhem in that state capitol building? Not from reading anything in my paper! No, I had to learn about it from those guys in Roslyn. I'm sure even you have heard of them—*USA Today?*"

Julius made another attempt to get the Editor's attention, "But, Boss, I think...", only to be ignored once more.

Wellen spoke as if Walsh hadn't said a word, "Hell, they didn't even have a reporter on the scene. They got the story from the police wires, a basic first grader tactic. Wait! Do you hear that? It sounds like the sound of laughter, coming from Roslyn. Now, do you get my drift? I think that those good brains of yours have started to slip south. You can bring that smart ass of yours back here, now!!"

Julius now realized that the pause here was only to gather new breath, he would wait until the steam stopped coming from the earpiece of the phone.

"You better pray that there is nothing in their edition tomorrow about a rival's "Ace" reporter being at the scene and never logging a word."

Julius finally got in a few words, "Boss, listen to me." He waited to see if he would be interrupted, but was able to continue. "You and I both know how that other paper goes for the headlines, tip of the iceberg information. The details come from digging deep. No, I didn't post an article about those deaths. Unfortunate as they may be, I thought they really only affected the local area and the family members. I see our paper as more than a body-count register."

Taking a second to get his own breath, Julius continued, "But, maybe that is not the case now. As I was saying earlier, I sent you some pictures that put the human element into those captions you read in the other paper."

He had finally gotten Wellen's interest. "What are you talking about? Hold on while I pull up your e-mail." There were a few moments of silence while Wellen checked his e-mails, found Julius' transmission and opened the attachment. Not unexpectedly, he saw a few dozen shots of Von Mumser meeting and greeting various Governors, State Legislators and the public in various states.

"Yeah, I see the pictures. Just what is so great about them? Looks like a lot of publicity shots to me."

Julius, being very proud of his discovery, explained, "Well, in a way yes. But, look at picture number seventeen." He waited while the Editor pulled up the picture and enlarged it to fill the screen.

Wellen commented, "Okay...Von Mumser and some dude. So what?"

Julius was really excited now. "That **dude** is one of the bodies they found in Trenton two weeks ago. I took many shots of the Chairman as he promoted his cause to the politicians and local citizens in each state. That guy was just one of many greetings that I took; but, as it turned out, he was also one of the three men that died that day."

Not getting a comment from the Editor at this point, Julius said, "And Boss, look at picture number fifty-one."

Again, Julius waited for Wellen to bring up the picture and enlarge it on the screen. "Yeah, I see it. What are they doing? Shaking hands?"

Julius corrected him, "Nay, I think the Chairman is giving the guy his business card."

Wellen cut in, "Wait, are you saying this guy also bought the farm? That this is one of the guys in Atlanta?"

With a little pride in his voice, Julius replied, "Yes that was one of the guys the Chairman spoke with yesterday. You see Boss; I don't think any other reporter has pictures like these. Those two guys looked fine, healthy and happy to me, yet just a few hours after these shots—BAM!!—They keel over, dead, reasons unknown. No, that's not true. The reason being no pulse, they stopped breathing. Cause? Now that's the unknown here."

Carrying on by his sense of discovery, he added, "I am going over the remaining digitals that I haven't deleted yet to see if any of the other dead men got in the way of the lens. Boss, I'm not sure if these deaths have any connection to each other or if someone is killing these people to try to sabotage Von Mumser's cause. I just know that I need to stay here, or wherever it is that the Chairman is. You never know. If the statehood issue flops, we just might be on the trail of something else. So, what do you say? Stay or go?"

Wellen now saw Julius' information in a different light. If the Kid was correct, then maybe there was some nut case out there, somehow getting to people and doing it in the background of the Chairman's visits. Well, it was worth thinking about, stranger things have happened. If this was the case, then it was time for the *Daily* to be in on the breaking edge. He told Julius, "Okay, okay. You make a good argument. You can stay, for the time being. If nothing interesting starts to develop, politically or otherwise, I'm pulling in your chain—got that?"

Julius felt like he had just won a major battle, worn out but victorious. "Yes Sir, Mr. Wellen, Boss Sir. Loud and clear. Gotta go now, there are lots of shots to review and the Chairman is on the road again later today. He is going home for a couple of days before heading back out to his next stomping grounds, Connecticut. I will come by the office and show you what I have. Then I thought I would do some research on the Connecticut Governor's political views—sort of like trying to guess if he will be in favor of the Chairman's cause, or not." Trying for humor and for some forgiveness with the Editor, Julius tagged on, "There should not be any problem getting into the office tomorrow. There is no nasty weather expected—something I got from our paper! So, I should see you about ten in the morning, okay?"

Wellen replied, "Yeah, I'll be here. And, Kid, don't delete any more pictures. Bring them all in. If that means you will need new cartridges for the next trip—so be it. This way I get to see what you think is so important." Replacing the headset, the Editor smiled. He loved it when something pulled at his detective sense.

At the other end, as Julius hung up, he made a mental note to review all of his pictures from the past few weeks. There were literally hundreds of shots of the Chairman with thousands of people. He then consoled himself with the thought that he had not deliberately been looking for other people's faces, just looking for good PR shots. It was possible to have overlooked some pictures that may have contained the dead guys. Here was just another reporter's lesson gone awry with him—not paying attention to the entire scene and only the subject of moment. Picking up his camera to start reviewing the frames he gave himself a mental smack on the head and a determination to do better before the Editor moved him to the Astrology or Cartoon section.

CHAPTER V

January 4, 2015
WTRU Talk Radio Studio
Peachtree Plaza
Atlanta, Georgia

At nine a.m., the syndicated morning talk radio show from Atlanta began. "Rise and shine Peach State, and all of our wonderful other listeners across the country. This is January 4th, 2015 and I'm your host, Bubba Meisah, here at WTRU." Bubba went on to explain the topic of discussion for this day's segment.

"As most people here know, two days ago four bodies were found scattered throughout our state capitol building. That's right, right here in Atlanta. While not a lot of information has been released, we do know that all the men were local residents. No cause for the deaths has been released."

Bubba paused a moment for effect and then continued, "So far, the police have declined interviews, stating they are still investigating the crime scene. I say, so far, but that is about to change today with one of our guests. Here at WTRU we believe you, the public, need to know what happened at the capitol. Especially as it appears Atlanta may not be the only location of these mysterious deaths. Seems that both Pennsylvania and New Jersey also had unusual deaths at their state buildings recently.

Folks, today we are fortunate indeed. We have two special guests with us in the studio. Two people who may be able to provide some insight on these mysterious incidents. Especially if these deaths are going to pose any form of health hazard to the general public."

Again, Bubba paused for impact before continuing. "Our first guest is none other than our own esteemed Chief of Police, Hank Sager. Also of equal prominence is our second guest, Ms. Maris Ayin, Regional Superintendent, here in Atlanta, for the Center for Disease Control, better known as the CDC."

Hank was seated across the control panel from Bubba, with his earphones in place ready for the program. He was listening to the DeeJay prattle on about the reasons for this particular program. Hank did not want to be interviewed about the bodies in the state building until he felt he had something of value to release. He certainly did not want to be on a talk radio program. He was here at the direction of Governor Froehlich.

Hank ensured that the local law enforcement unions always supported the Governor's initiatives and re-election efforts. If Hank had any conflict of opinion with the Governor, he kept it to himself. His public statements always aligned with the Governor's viewpoint or interpretation. That was how Hank saw his duty today, as a guest speaker on this talk show. He was being the peacemaker between a potentially irate public and the Governor's desire to down play any negative impact from these recent deaths on Froehlich's ability to govern and safeguard the citizens of Georgia.

Hank was determined to pull the plug on any spotlight this talk-jockey tried to shine on Georgia. His second, and equally important, aim today was to assure his wife and two young sons that as long as he was the Chief of Police, the youth of Atlanta could rely on him to keep them safe.

As Bubba spoke Hank's name, the Chief returned to the present in full force. "Chief Sager, I want to thank you for taking the time to be here with us today."

Rather than express a delight that he did not feel, the Chief nodded his head at the host and stated, "No problem."

"So, Chief," Bubba began, "Is there any truth to the rumor that these deaths may be connected with the recent deaths in New Jersey and Pennsylvania?"

Not one for long-winded replies, Hank's was monosyllabic, "No."

Taken aback by the short comment, Bubba asked another question, more generic in theory, hoping for more in the way of conversation. "Chief Sager, do you think someone out there may have a grudge, or a vendetta, against government buildings, or people who visit these buildings?"

Ever mindful of the Governor's directive to minimize worry and fear amongst the citizens, Hank made a snorting sound before informing the host and the listening audience that these types of mishaps happened all the time across the country. But, for whatever reason, maybe lack of more important national events, this one occurrence in Atlanta had captured the headlines.

Hank expanded his explanation, "This is not a daily happening here in Georgia. In fact, according the latest Law Enforcement and Crime Data, our state is in the bottom third for per-capita crimes."

Now this was more the type of dialogue Bubba was after. He asked for more, "Really, Chief? And where do New Jersey and Pennsylvania fall out in this list? I mean, are they higher up the line with more per-capita crimes?"

Hank hesitated a moment before answering, "Well, no. But what does that have to do with anything? Georgia law enforcement has gained a lot of ground in reducing the crime rate in the past few years. I don't know about those other states. I don't know if their crime rate has been declining, like here, staying steady or growing. You would have to interview their law enforcement. I can only speak about right here in Georgia."

Bubba continued as if the Chief had not spoken. "So, tell us Chief, do you happen to have the stats on the number of murders? I was under the impression that Georgia's murder rate was declining. But these four bodies might prove that wrong. Does Pennsylvania or New Jersey have more murders than Georgia?"

Bubba sensed that he was about to get the type of excited response he was hoping for as Hank immediately reacted. "Whoa, what are you saying? What are you trying to imply? We know there was no foul play with guns or knives. The police found no evidence of any physical violence. Are you talking about some type of chemical violence?

Because, again, the police found no evidence of entry marks or wounds. So, who said anything about murder?"

Deciding it was time to shed the spotlight, and hoping to redirect the line of question and interest, Hank turned to the other guest seated to his right and asked, "Hey, Ms. CDC Lady, do you have any proof that these guys were murdered? In fact, do you have any evidence that you **can** share?"

Maris Ayin had been quietly following the back and forth banters between the show's host and the Chief of Police. Other than the location of the CDC headquarters being in Atlanta, she saw no explanation for her guest appearance. The CDC had only been involved in the "capitol deaths," as they were beginning to be called, since yesterday. All of one day. The coroner reports were not even available from Pennsylvania or New Jersey yet. She did have the local preliminary report from the Atlanta coroner; but nothing to indicate suspicious occurrences.

Maris was the first black female to become a regional superintendent for the CDC. At forty-three, Maris had retained her youthful beauty. An attractive, physically fit woman, with shiny black straight hair shot through with auburn highlights, her skin was flawlessly smooth, and her eyes were the most unusual shade of amber, reminding people of the inner shine of that semi-precious gem. Ever conscientious of herself being viewed as a symbol of the agency, Maris emanated a professional aura that told all she came in contact with that she was one smart cookie. The projection was that she not only knew her subject, but she was more than willing to share that knowledge with anyone who asked.

Maris holds to a new school of thought that knowledge is power, but only if you spread it around. To her way of thinking, someone that holds vital information to him-or-herself, in the belief that it will make them more valuable, was taking risks with the lives of infected patients. She does not deal well with these types of individuals. On those rare occasions when she found herself able to relax and chat with others, her smile totally transformed her appearance. She smiled with her entire face, displaying a full set of pearly white teeth, a set of dimples in her cheeks, a twinkle in her eyes, and friendliness that erases years from her features.

With eighteen years of employment at the center she was well positioned, being very knowledgeable and highly credentialed, to become the agency's next director in the not too distant future. The current director, Tom Pearson, had started hinting about retirement. He jokingly told Maris that it was time for him to really enjoy his bride, referring to his wife of more than forty years. Tom also wanted to spoil his grandchildren, something he was not able to do with his own children.

Maris, a Phi Beta Kappa alumnus from the University of Mississippi, Medical Center, School of Pathology, earned her Ph.D. in Emerging Infectious Disease, School of Pathology and Preventive Medicine, from the Uniformed Services University of the Health Sciences, in Bethesda, Maryland. It was while attending this prestigious learning institution that Maris was introduced to and enthralled by the research opportunities provided by the Center for Disease Control. Rather than work on "what could be's," she wanted to dedicate her time on the sudden emergence of unknown infections. Working under the pressure of time sensitive limitations always brought out the crusader in Maris.

Rallying to the present challenge she detected in the Chief's tone, Maris informed him, "Actually, we are in the initial stages of our involvement with these deaths. As you know, Chief Sager, our assistance was only requested yesterday. As I recall, that request came from Governor Froehlich's office."

Not stopping, she added, "We have not yet found any evidence that points conclusively to a means, or method, for the number of deaths. These men were seemingly healthy individuals. The anomaly lies in them all having died at approximately the same time and in the same place."

She quickly added, "Let me ease any fears of the listening public. Whatever the final analysis is from our investigation, it will not be of a contagious nature. The air in the capitol building was tested for any airborne hazardous particles. The air was clean. There is nothing in the ventilation of the building to case a health alert. As to how, or even if, these deaths are in any way medically related to the deaths in other state capitol buildings, I cannot comment. We are only just gathering the information from those locations."

Bubba sensed that he would only be covering the same ground so he asked his guests if either had a theory on why these individuals were affected or what they thought may be a common thread. Neither guest offered any helpful information.

Bubba decided to get the audience involved at this point; hoping to stimulate the topic into another segment after the CDC investigation was completed. He announced that the lines were open for listener participation and provided the one-eight hundred telephone number. He stated that not only were questions for the guests welcomed, but if anyone had any information, or even a theory, to call.

As only one line began the call ins, a caller wanting to know how to apply for a job at the police department, Bubba announced a break in the program for commercial announcements.

CHAPTER VI

January 4, 2015
Yale Professor Harvey Cohen's Home
New Haven, Connecticut

Harvey Cohen, forty-three, Professor of Economics at Yale University, was trying once again, not to burn the over easy eggs in the frying pan.

A recent widower, he was also the father of Brandon and Jodie. As he rushed between the refrigerator, the counter top, the stove, and the kitchen table, he told his son, "Brandon, please tell Jodie breakfast is ready. And do me a favor; tell her now while the eggs are warm and not burnt."

Brandon, twelve, was listening to a talk radio program and did not respond. Always a quiet child, Brandon had buried himself in his books and studies since his mother died in an automobile crash nine months ago. Harvey was concerned that Brandon was hiding himself in books and computer programs as a way of dealing with his mother's passing. Being the younger child, Brandon received most of the attention and affection from Laura. Harvey quite understood how much Brandon missed her. But his worry was that his son was avoiding interacting with other people as a way to protect his feelings, in case something should happen to them. It was a living and learning experience for Harvey as he saw how differently children dealt with the death of a loved one.

While Brandon hid in his world of academia, Jodie, fourteen, had become the woman of the house. She managed the grocery shopping, the laundry, and the housekeeping. Not now, or ever, had she been an early riser and was very content to have her father deal with the morning meals. Jodie had a healthy fascination with all things teenage. This included the love of loud music, teen idols, dancing, the latest fashions, and all things electronic. She literally spent the majority of any given day on either the computer or the cell phone.

Since the automobile accident, she saw herself as a stand-in mother for Brandon. She helped to select his clothes, walked him to school, and met him at home after school. She saw Brandon's withdrawal and took the time to help him with his homework, to instruct him on new computer games and to just talk with him about everyday things. To her, Brandon seemed determined to erect walls around his heart. And Jodie was just as determined to ensure there was a sibling connection that let him know the rest of the family was here and loved him.

"Brandon, NOW, Please!" The raised tone of his father's voice got Brandon's attention.

Turning his head from the radio to face his father, he said, "Dad, have you heard about these strange deaths in some state capitols?"

"Yeah, I read about the ones yesterday in Georgia. Also about some deaths a couple of weeks ago in New Jersey. I know that it must seem unusual to have several deaths on the same day in a state building. But, it is not so unusual to have several unexplained deaths on any given day in any one place."

Taking a breath and pausing for effect, Harvey looked directly at his son and said, "If you want to continue this conversation you will have to go get your sister first. I know you, my man; once you start in on a topic, you lose all track of time—something we have a limited supply of first thing in the morning. So, Jodie first, talk second, got it?"

With a frown on his face, Brandon appeared to think through his options. Reaching a decision, he smiled at his dad and got up to go get his sister. As he left the room, he called over his shoulder, "Okay, Dad, but I do have a thought I want to talk about with you."

While Brandon was out of the room, Harvey put out the place settings. Before he could finish dishing out the food, Brandon was back. As Brandon sat down at the kitchen table, he continued the earlier conversation.

"Dad, the talk show this morning is from Atlanta, Georgia. That is the same place where they had the deaths yesterday. But, they also said there were deaths in the capitol buildings of Pennsylvania and New Jersey. Do know if there were any deaths in Delaware?"

"No, I don't know Bran, I don't remember reading about anything strange there. Why do you ask?"

"Well, it is just kind of odd that these deaths seem to be happening in states that were from the original colonies. I know because this year we have been learning about the American Revolution in Social Studies. But, you know, something else is odd to me."

"What's odd to you?" Harvey asked as he poured orange juice into three glasses.

"You see, unless there have been other deaths in state capitols that haven't been reported, these people are dying in a sort of order."

Harvey stopped drinking his orange juice and looked questioningly at his son. "What kind of order do you mean, Bran?"

"You know Dad; it's just odd that the people happen to be dying in the states that were the original thirteen colonies. And, you know, if there were any people in Delaware, that would be, like, more in line with what I am thinking. That would mean that first there was Delaware, then Pennsylvania, then New Jersey and now Georgia. That's a way cool idea, huh, Dad?"

"Well, I have to admit, I have not given it much thought. And, as I said, I don't know anything about Delaware. What are the people on the talk show saying?"

Shrugging his shoulders, Brandon said, "Other than the top cop snapping at everyone, not much. The lady from the CDC says she does not have anything to say yet because today is her first day on the case. But, Dad, you know how government people can be. You always say that they only let us know what they want us to know, right?"

A bit embarrassed that his son had picked up his distrust of governmental systems and people, Harvey tried to correct this perception, "Yeah, well, I know I have said that, but you have to understand where I'm coming from. I don't mean that you shouldn't trust all government people all the time. I know that your mom and I have told you, since you could understand, that the police are your friends. Right?"

Brandon nodded his head in agreement.

"And that the schools around here are the best in the state, right?"

Again Brandon nodded his agreement.

"That's because the mayor believes that those taxes collected for the school system should really go to school improvements. I'm sorry to say that my distrust of the government and its processes is probably at a higher level than that lady from the CDC."

Eager to change the subject, Harvey asked, "Brandon, I know you like listening to the radio. What has caught your interest about this one? Usually you listen to the sports programs, right? So why this one?"

Brandon, holding a slice of toast between his hands, took a bite, shrugged his shoulders, and mumbled around the food, "I dunno, maybe 'cause of the talk bout the states." He cleared his throat to continue, "And maybe, because of my school lessons, they just seemed interesting to me."

Becoming more animated, Brandon hurried on, "Dad, the talk show guy said if anyone had any questions to call the show. I wrote down the toll-free number. Would it be okay if I called? That way I could, like, ask my question about Delaware. After all, the worse that they can say is no—or—they don't know. What do you say, Dad, can I? Please?"

In a youthful attempt at a bribe, he added, "And I'll help clean up the dishes right after I call. That way Jodie can take her time eating and we can leave for school at the same old time. That sounds fair, doesn't it?"

Trying not to smile, Harvey gave in. "Okay, but if the line is busy, we clear the table and go, agreed?"

"Sure Dad. But, you have to be fair about this. If the line is busy on the first try, I should be able to try a second time. After that, if I can't get in, we leave. But, if I can't talk with the radio guy then I guess I don't have to clean up the kitchen. I mean, the deal was a clean up for a talk, right?"

Actually pushing his tongue against the inside of his cheek, Harvey fought to control his smile. "Technically, I think you have it backwards guy. If I recall our talk, the deal was a clean up for letting you call the radio station. Not IF you got through, or, IF you talked to anyone. But, I guess two tries is okay—go ahead."

Getting up from his kitchen chair, Brandon made a right-handed triumphant pumping motion in the air. As he headed for the telephone, he crows, "Yes!!! Thanks Dad! Don't worry; I know I will get through."

Whether a prophecy or not, Brandon was able to get through, on the second try.

CHAPTER VII

January 4, 2015
WTRU Talk Radio Studio
Peachtree Plaza
Atlanta, Georgia

While Brandon remained on hold, the host was beginning the last segment of the program.
"Welcome back to the morning talk hour with me, your host, Bubba Meisah. It seems that today's guests have generated some interest from you, the listening audience. The phone lines are just about all lit up. Let's see what the people have to say."
Glancing at a cue card provided by the program's assistant, Bubba continued, "Our first caller is Harriett, with two Ts, from Hagerstown, Maryland."
Pushing the first blinking light on the telephone control panel, Bubba started the conversation,
"Good Morning Harriett, welcome to the show. This is Bubba Meisah. What's on your mind?"
Expecting a reply, Bubba frowned when nothing happened; getting nothing but blank air.
"Hello, Harriett, with two Ts, are you there?"
Another few seconds of blank time, then a female voice asked, "Um, hello? Is this Bubba Meisah?"
"Yes, Ma'am, it is. How can I help you?"
"Oh, hi, my name is Harriett...with two Ts."
Yes, Ma'am, I know."
"Most people spell my name with one T. That's why I always have to tell folks about the two Ts."

Grinning at the explanation, Bubba prompted the caller, "Yes, Ma'am. I can understand the mistake. You have something to say about today's subject?"

"I'm calling from Hagerstown, Maryland. That's where I live."

"Yes, Ma'am, I know."

Bubba gave a questioning look at his two guests as he sensed that perhaps the caller was either very nervous or a bit on the slow side. He decided to give the caller some encouragement.

"Well, Harriett, with two Ts, from Hagerstown, Maryland, what would you like to say to our guests? I'm sure it is important or you would not have taken the time to call. Speak to me."

Harriett, hesitantly, started her comments, "Well, um, it just seems odd to me that all these guys are dying in government owned buildings."

Not saying anything else and thinking she was waiting for an acknowledgement, Bubba prompted her, "Yes?"

"Well, uh, I was just wondering, uh, if maybe this is some sort of, uh, government action…the killing of these men."

That remark had Chief Sager sitting up in his chair, not liking the idea of a conspiracy, and he said, "Who said anything about murder? We don't even know why these folks died. What makes you think that the government would be behind these deaths?"

After another few second Harriett replied, "Well, it seems to me that maybe these men were like, uh, some kind of bad guys. You know, thieves or murderers and this way the taxpayers would not have to spend tons of money on trials that slick city lawyers would get them out of. Then they would be free to do more crimes. I think the government was acting in our best interest."

Bubba made eye contact with the Chief and tapped a finger on the side of his head to let the Chief know his opinion of the caller. He then lowered his finger and drew an imaginary line across his throat to let his guests know the call was over.

Disconnecting the line, Bubba told the listening audience, "Yes, well, thank you Harriett, with two Ts, from Hagerstown. I am sure your comments were carefully thought out before your call."

He again looked at his guests while shaking his head from side to side.

"Okay, while that was very informative, I am afraid it did not raise any questions or comments for our studio guests."

Looking again at his prompt card on the next caller, Bubba continued, "Caller Number Two is Brian from right here in our own backyard, Atlanta." Pushing the phone line to connect, he stated, "Talk to me Brian. What's on your mind?"

"Yes. Good morning Mr. Meisah, Chief Sager and Ms. Ayin. My question is for the Police Chief. Chief Sager, sir, I was wondering what are the requirements to apply for the police academy and do you recommend that form of law enforcement as a good job career?"

Happy to engage in a subject not related to the program's main theme, the Chief launched into a recruiting dialogue, honed over the years, to guarantee an enthusiastic enrollment. The caller was very pleased with the information and told the Chief he was going to visit the academy administration office today and disconnected.

The Chief was feeling rather pleased with himself. He thought that if he ever left the force, he could be the number one car salesman in Atlanta, Georgia. He was even more elated when he glanced at the station wall clock and realized there were only a few more minutes before the program was over.

Bubba was determined to have one serious call-in conversation before completing today's program.

"Okay callers, time is running out and I know that some of you have some great questions for our quests. So, I'll tell you what we are going to do. We will continue to take calls on the air. If we cannot get to everyone currently on hold…don't hang up. We will take your calls off line. We will provide your comments and questions to our quests for reply. Then, we will air the information during a future segment of the show. Do you hear me callers? If you are holding, please don't hang up…we will be talking with every one of you."

Again more looking at his cue cards, Bubba continued, "Our next caller is Brandon from New Haven, Connecticut. Speak o me Brandon…But you may have to talk fast man, we are just about out of time."

Bubba blinked twice and gave the caller his full attention when he realized that Brandon was more boy than man.

"Hello, Mr. Meisah? My name is Brandon and I have a question for the police officer. Sir, I was wondering if there were any unexplained deaths at the capitol in Delaware—or—in any other capitol building on the east coast."

Chief Sager quickly replied, "No, son, none that I am aware of. I assume you mean recently. Because I would think that just about every state building has had one or more unexplained deaths at some time during its existence."

It was clear that this was not the answer that Brandon was looking for. "Oh, uh, are you sure?"

"Well, this is the first time anyone has asked me this question. So, no, I cannot say for certain. Is there some reason that you want to know about Delaware?" was Chief Sager's explanation.

"Well, it was just a thought I had when I was listening to the talk on the show. It is not just Delaware that I am asking about, but all of the original thirteen states. The only states that were mentioned on the show are from the original colonies.

You see, just before winter break, we were studying the American Revolution in Social Studies and the three states you are talking about today; Pennsylvania, Georgia, and New Jersey are three of the original thirteen. So, I was just wondering if there were any unusual deaths, recently, in any of the other ten state capitols that formed the union. I only mentioned Delaware because it was the first state to sign."

Afraid that he might get cut off, Brandon paused for breath and then rushed to continue, "Is there anyway that you can check to see if any people were found dead at the other capitols?"

Maris, listening to the conversation was reminded of her own budding genius at home, eight year old Joseph.

After twelve years of marriage, the blessing of her life entered the world eight years ago in the form of her son, Joseph. Joseph was showing signs of becoming an electronic wizard. He amazed everyone with his creations made from parts of toys and discarded appliances. Maris smiled as she recalled telling Joseph his smarts must be something he inherited from his father, because his beautiful features definitely came from her side of the family.

Maris knows how tenacious Joseph can be when he was concentrating on something. And that same level of seriousness was what she was hearing in Brandon's voice. It was a genuine quest for information, not just some morbid appeal for gory details. She also had the urge to talk with Brandon. To find out what made him settle on the thirteen original states.

She rationalized that maybe there was something valuable in the thought process of the young that adults tended to miss after too many years of "logic." Besides, she told herself, the autopsies were not completed yet, so any new idea was always a good one.

She leaned forward in her chair and, quite out of character for her, cut into the conversation between the Chief and Brandon, "Brandon, I'm Maris Ayin from the Center for Disease Control. Would it be okay if I talk with you, off line, after the program is over? The show is about to end and I have some thoughts about your idea that I think we can discuss. Would that be okay with you?"

A very happy Brandon agreed with to the talk and gladly gave Maris his home telephone number when she asked for it. Brandon promised to stay by the telephone as he hung up and turned to look at his father with a definite smug expression on his face.

"Hey, Dad! Guess what! That CDC lady, Maris, wants to talk with me!" Brandon announced as he patted himself on the chest. He then made a fisted pumping motion in the air. "Yes! She wants to talk to me. ME!! Brandon Cohen, Nerd Supreme! She thinks I have a good idea. Can you believe it? This is soooo cool. Ya-Hoo!!"

Watching his son, Harvey's heart achingly warred with his pride in his enthusiasm and his wish that Laura could be here to share the moment. Gathering his emotions under control, he smiled as he walked over and patted his son on the back.

"Yeah, Bran, it feels great, doesn't it, to have someone besides your family tell you how smart you are? So…now what happens? Are you supposed to just wait for Ms. Ayin to call you? Do you know when she may be calling? I'm only asking because we have to leave for school pretty soon, or risk being late."

That comment brought Brandon back to earth with a thud. "Leave for school? No way Dad! I mean, can't we be a little late, just this once? How often do we get to talk with important people involved in something special? Oh, please, Dad, just this one time?"

Torn between supporting his son's interest and the need to maintain their daily schedule, Harvey offered a compromise. "I'll tell you what. We still have about fifteen minutes before we absolutely have to leave. Well, at least I have to leave then in order to make my first lecture. So, if Ms. Ayin hasn't called by them, I'll have Jodie stay with you for another thirty minutes. I'll even leave cab fare for you two to get to school on time. But, if there is no call by then, you must leave for school and Ms. Ayin will either leave a message or have to call back. Deal?"

"Deal. And Dad thanks. I really appreciate your understanding."

"No problem, son. I do understand how important this is for you. And, that reminds me. There is something important coming out of this for me too."

Waiting to get his son's attention, he added, "The dishes, remember? They will not wash themselves. You can do that while you are waiting for the call."

Brandon nodded his agreement as he went off to clean up the kitchen. Harvey went into the study to talk with Jodie and arranged for the taxi. The noise in the kitchen told Harvey that Brandon was rushing through his chore. When Harvey returned to the kitchen, he saw Brandon sitting in the chair by the telephone, staring at the instrument as if willing it to ring. He didn't have to wait long. A few minutes later, he received the call from Maris.

"Hello, Brandon? Maris Ayin here. I would like to thank you for your call to the station this morning. Not a lot of people your age...about twelve or thirteen years old?" Maris stopped and waited for a reply from Brandon, who confirmed her guess of twelve years old.

"Well, not many twelve year olds would have the confidence to call a talk show. You remind me of my own son, Joseph. He is eight years old and very smart. That's a compliment for you Brandon. I'll bet you are a top notch student. Am I right?"

Awkwardly Brandon acknowledged being on the honor roll.

Maris was pleased that her assumption about him was correct and she told him so. She then asked Brandon what made him come up with the idea that the strange deaths were related to the thirteen original states.

Brandon explained that he was not really sure if only the thirteen states were involved, since he doesn't know if there were like situations in any other state. But, he told Maris that if those deaths were only in the three states that were talked about on the radio program, then those would be related to the original states. Brandon asked her if she knew of anything like this in any of the other ten original states. He explained that he only asked about Delaware because it was the first to sign the Declaration of Independence. He again asked Maris if she knew of any deaths in Delaware.

Maris was impressed with Brandon's thought process. She was not aware of any other unexplained cases, as this was her first day of involvement and only knew of those events in Pennsylvania, New Jersey, and Georgia. She promised Brandon to check on the other ten original states. She also promised that whatever she learned, she would call him back and share the information. Before she hung up, she gave Brandon her office telephone number. Saying goodbye, the telephone call was terminated.

With her hand still on the telephone cradle, an idea came to Maris. Smiling to herself, she took a small notepad from her purse and wrote down the name of someone she knew would be glad to help with her investigation...Stella Vega.

Chapter VIII

January 5, 2015
FBI Building
Washington,, DC

Stella Vega, profiler extraordinaire, or so her reputation went, was entering her office on the fourth floor when her cell phone started ringing. Smiling to herself, she reached for the cell before the theme music from *Law and Order* drew attention. She was an avid fan and tried not to miss a show. Looking at the number on the ID screen, she glanced heavenward before answering.

"Hi, Mom. How are you? Since it is seven a.m. here in Washington; that makes it, what?...five a.m. in Albuquerque? This really must be important."

As she listened to her mother, Stella's stance stiffened slightly. At thirty-two, Stella was the bane of her mother's existence. Or so she told Stella at least once during every conversation. Mrs. Vega has made it her number one priority to see her daughter happily married. Of the six Vega children, Stella, child number five, was the only one still single. In her mother's view, this was a sign of failure, for Mrs. Vega, not for Stella. In her mother's cultural background, a successful life meant getting married, having children, seeing them married and being surrounded by a large number of grandchildren. That meant that the children must live close by and come to the house at least once a week, with the grandchildren. That is what women did.

Stella knew that her mother loved her, as did the rest of her family. She also knew that it hurt her mother and surprised her siblings when she decided to go to college and then, after graduation, when she pursued her desire to become an FBI agent. That career meant moving away from the home. Stella saw the move as a way to find herself, to be herself, and to even be able to sneeze without having half a dozen people hand her tissues and ask if she was getting a cold.

Stella was proud of herself, her career, and her accomplishments. Her profession allowed her to live on her own, something she only dreamed about when growing up in a three bedroom house with seven other people. She owned a two bedroom condominium in Annandale, Virginia and one of those bedrooms was used as an exercise room. No roommates for Stella.

The cost of this freedom meant allowing for, at least, one call a day from home. This was a price that Stella was glad to pay. Deep inside she loved her family and these daily chats kept her involved in everything that she was not at home to be able to see and hear. The one drawback, and the reason she believed she was her mother's burden, was her insistence on not rushing to marry someone her mother has just met. Stella firmly believed that if she was destined to be married, it would happen in its own way and time. That thought brought her back to the present and what her mother was saying. Stella felt the need to cut the conversation short.

"Mom? Mom? Listen to me. I really don't mean to be disrespectful. And I am not…being disrespectful, I mean. But, Mom, you really have to stop this matchmaking. Mom, I love you, you know that. But, I am at work and do not have the time to go through this now. Please tell Mrs. Guareno that I'm flattered she wants me to meet her nephew. And, please explain that I work out of town and am not available at this time. Can you do this for me Mom? Please?"

The next comment from her mother made Stella stiffen even more. "Mother, I don't care if the man is coming to Washington for business. I do not have time. Do you hear me? No time. I am working on several cases that require all my time."

Stella took a moment to calm down, and Mrs. Vega continued her end of the talk.

"Mom, I am sorry that you gave him my telephone number. I will just to have to explain to him when, if, he actually calls. Sorry Mom, I really have to go. I am at my office and there are several people here. Hug and kiss Papa for me. I love you. Bye."

She snapped the cell phone closed before her mother could go on. She then switched the ringer to vibrate so she could honestly tell her mother that she did not hear the phone ring when she called back. She never wanted to lie to her mother. Just as she was being honest when she said there were people at work; co-workers, law enforcement personnel, custodial staff, etc. She was careful not to say those people were *in* her office. No one would be there until she unlocked her door.

Entering her work area, she hung her raincoat on the coat rack standing in the corner next to the one window overlooking Pennsylvania Avenue and she glanced out the window. At this hour in the morning, the traffic had yet to reach top rush hour volume. The light rain this morning put a coating on the roads that gave everything a shiny clean appearance. She was always humbled to think that she was here in this city, the seat of the American governmental world. Everyday she was thankful that she had the opportunity to try to make America safer for at least one person, if not an entire community somewhere in the country.

Taking a deep breath to clear her thoughts, she moved between the window and her desk to power up her computer. As she pushed the start button, she noticed the blinking light on her telephone voice mail. Sitting down, she placed her purse in a desk drawer and dialed the access code to retrieve her messages. There were a total of three messages. One was from a coworker wanting information on a case they were both involved with. She jotted down the requested data in order to send the work electronically when she could access her computer files. The second call was an agency generated announcement about upcoming system maintenance and potential disruptions during the upcoming weekend.

The third call was from a CDC superintendent, Maris Ayin, that Stella had worked with on several cases. She noticed that Maris called at about nine o'clock last night. She made a mental note to give Maris her cell phone number. Stella liked Maris, for both her professionalism and her pleasing personality. Stella felt that anyone having Maris as a friend could consider themselves lucky. In Stella's experience, top leaders in any organization tended to have an exaggerated sense of self. Maris was a lovely people oriented person. Maris cared, about what she does and the people she comes in contact with.

Stella decided to make Maris her first response. Dialing Maris' telephone number she hoped that seven-thirty in the morning was not too early to call her office. Things tended to start a little later in the morning in the southern states. Her concern proved a mute point when Maris answered the phone on the second ring.

"Maris Ayin here. How may I help you?"

Smiling at the familiar warmth in the voice as it came across the line, Stella replied, "Maris, this is Stella. And, actually, the question is how can I help you?"

Knowing that Maris would take a few social moments before getting to the reason for the call, Stella waited and knew it could not be too serious a matter for the call when she heard a short giggle on the other end.

"Stella thanks for calling back so quickly. How have you been? Still single? Or has your mother finally found Mr. Wonderful?"

"No, no Prince Charming yet. But, that doesn't stop Mom from continuing the search."

Maris heard the frustration in Stella's voice. She envisioned Stella as she last saw her, last year when they worked together on a case involving some weirdo who thought he had discovered a spray to eliminate the common cold. What he had actually concocted was a spray that manifested nasal sores that dripped dangerous acid into the stomach lining. Several people actually died from the application of that spray.

That is what got her and Stella into the scenario of tracking down this would be Dr. Salk as he randomly visited the homeless on the streets or in the shelters to provide his cure while people were sleeping. Rather than seeing the homeless as persons down on their luck, he saw them as readily available lab rats.

. Stella was a beautiful woman who walked with an air of confidence. Standing five feet six inches, she had olive skin, thick dark hair, black eyes and a sleek body honed by countless hours of physical fitness. Throughout their working encounters, regardless of the location, Stella maintained a professional demeanor. Even when some of the local law enforcement guys were more captivated by her classical Latin beauty than by the reason for her being in their jurisdiction.

"Stella, my girl, if you are still content in your own skin, then I am happy for you."

Maris waited a few seconds to change the mood and tone of her talk. When she continued, it was with the sound of her professional side.

"Stella, I know you are aware of these unexplained sudden deaths that recently occurred in at least three state capitol buildings. Today I was a guest on the Bubba Meisah radio talk show discussing potential reasons for these occurrences.

One of the call ins was a young man from Connecticut. He has an interesting theory about how the events are happening. He originally asked if there were any similar deaths in Delaware. Then he expanded that query to the ten other of the original thirteen states. To his way of thinking, since the current deaths have all happened in Pennsylvania, New Jersey and Georgia, he wondered if something was going down in the founding states.

I don't know of any such incidents. But, I was hoping that you, with your connections, might be able to check it out. It would be worth a shot to see if anything unusual has happened. But, Stella, I would be interested to know if this type of situation has happened anywhere in the country, not just the first thirteen states. Do you think you might have the time to check your systems for me?"

"Not a problem, Maris. Can do, easy. What time frame for the search do you have in mind?"

Maris was very pleased with the ready cooperation. "Well, considering that the three situations we know about happened over a three week period; how about looking at the three months prior to that time? Maybe starting at the beginning of September up until now. Would that take a long time?"

Stella grinned at the worry she heard in Maris' voice. "Lady, you seem to have forgotten, you are talking to the FBI. Sometimes that means Factual Browsing Instantly. Seems you have hit on one of those moments. Lucky you. I'll set up a search query right away and, with our usual efficiency, we should have the results in about one hour. Now, would you like a side order of analysis with that? If you do, that will take about another hour. It's your call."

Maris quickly accepted the offer and informed Stella that she was eagerly awaiting the results. To ensure that she did not miss the telephone call, she gave Stella her cell phone number. Stella returned the gesture, for any future needs. At this point they said their good byes and disconnected.

Stella immediately input the search requests and directed the results to both herself and her office assistant. After all, two brains were always better than one. While waiting for the information she emailed the files that her coworker's voice message requested.

Then she did a small inquiry of her own on the three states' incidents. It only takes a few minutes and she had all the available information. A few facts immediately came to her attention. One, all the victims were male. In Stella's mind, unless there was a valid reason for an unexpected situation, the person, or persons, involved was either the victim or the criminal. Two, they were all Caucasian, at least by the sound of the names and their physical appearances.

She started making some notes for further investigation. *Cause of death? Any connection between victims? Similarity with medic al problems—employment—hobbies—outside organizations—religion—credit card Company—school—military? Same day of occurrence travels: mass transportation—air, rail, bus?*

Pausing after these notes, she acknowledged there was always the random aspect to consider. Random was what intrigued her the most. Random was such a dubious word to her way of thinking. In her experience, and from all the cases she studied, repeated crimes of violence were never *random*, never without an aim or purpose. At least in the mind of the perpetrator.

Senseless as the crimes may appear to the average citizen, there was always some method behind the madness. Discovering who the criminal was, what made him, or her, do what they do, how they do what they do, was what got Stella's mental juices flowing. She thoroughly enjoyed getting inside the minds of these people and thwarting them at their own game.

THE COALITION

The adrenaline flow sometimes had her taking on mannerisms she believed the criminal possessed. Some coworkers have nicknamed her Ms. Lon Chaney. When a really big case had been solved, she would take a few days off to clear her mind of the criminal invasion and return to her normal behavior.

Continuing with the random line of thought, she used another sheet of paper for those notes: *Inferiority complex?;* Avenging *ex-lover(s)?: too much variance; Unhappy Black—Hispanic-Asian?; Gung-Ho bill collector? Ha-ha but check financial status; Political rivals? Check voter registration; Check last wills—who wrote policies?; Why at state building that day?; Where born?; Age differences/similarities?; Sexual preferences?; Criminal Records?*

Taking another piece of paper, Stella headed this one with one word: WHO? She then sub-headed the sheet with Male on the left side and Female on the right side. Under male she noted: *Probably not—too neat, too quiet, no visible trauma, some victims large in body mass—no sign of confrontation, no use of obvious weapons.*

Then, under Female she noted: *Possibly for all the same reasons listed above for not being a male.*

Yet this did not feel like a feminine hand to Stella. Besides the fact that these men did not have any related outward features, thus taking away the theory of a jilted ex-lover seeking revenge, or any possible look-a-like mistaken identity factor. On the other side of the coin, the lack of physical violence did not point to a masculine influence.

Stella made some more notes for research:

Was there a connection to the heating products in the building? Any common custodial service? Any common construction crews? Any one person, or persons, at all the sites?

Another thought came to her: What type of person, or persons, would all the victims have trusted enough to allow close contact, at least close enough to have permitted access for some type of personal transmission or administration of something lethal? Stella completely rejected any acceptance of mass coincidental deaths. It just did not exist.

Stella was still going over her initial thoughts about the victims when her computer sounded the arrival of new email. It was the reply to her query. Opening the attached spreadsheet, she knew the analysis was not going to add any missing pieces to the current events. The incoming data showed four situations at state capitols during the three months prior to the Pennsylvania incident. Three scenarios did not result in any known deaths, but the fourth notation was one heart failure in Delaware on December 7th. Yes, this was one of the ten primary states under consideration, but one potentially valid heart attack was not outside the realm of reality. Yet, with all the other deaths, it was worth a further look.

Stella was going to let her assistant do any analysis anyway, for experience training. But she did not see a reason to delay her relating the information to Maris. Stella reached Maris on her cell phone. "Maris, the results are in and I have three nothing-significants and one possibility."

"Okay, Stella, I'm listening. Let me hear the findings, please."

"Well, on September 10th there was a woman who went into labor while visiting her state representative in Wisconsin. She had twins and all are fine. Then, on September 28th, there was a protest over building casinos in Tennessee. One man set himself on fire. They were able to extinguish the fire and hospitalize the fellow. He is in a burn unit in a psychiatric ward. Dramatic, but not in line with what we are looking for. Then, on November 22nd, there was an irate constituent in Rhode Island. He burst into the Governor's office and held him hostage, at gun point, for three hours. Seems he felt the Governor was personally responsible for the seizure of some of his agricultural supplies. The guy was growing marijuana in rows between his string beans and squash. After talks with a negotiator failed, they brought his son in and let him talk with the father. That's when the man surrendered and is still under arrest."

"Cute, Stella, real cute. Now tell me about the possibility, please."

"Okay, seems like our little Master Brandon had a lucky guess. On December 7th there was one death at the Delaware state capitol building. Reports say it was a sudden, fatal heart attack. The man was forty-three and touring the building with his wife and two children. Seems one child has political aspirations and they were there to see about applying for a summer government intern program. There was no known history of any heart problems, so it came as a complete surprise to the family. Now I know that this is only one incident. And one does not indicate a serial situation. But, in light of the other cases, I think it bears further investigation. What do you think?"

"I agree. Stella, I'm going to request the M.E.'s report on this guy. Would you be kind enough to fax me the information on this man? You can use my office fax number. And, Stella thanks for the attention and fast response. I'll let you now the results of all the cases. I'm going to give Brandon Cohen a call as soon as we finish. Speak to you soon. Bye."

After replacing the cradle onto the telephone, Stella went back over her notes and reviewed her options for further analyses. Knowing this would require a multi-state investigation, she immediately came up with the names of two FBI agents that would relish this type of challenge. Sal Caruso and Steve Woods. These were two New York City agents with bloodhound instincts. No job was too small and common or too big and bizarre for these guys. Stella looked up their office telephone numbers and called. Neither man was at his desk. Stella left a message for either of them to call, whenever they retrieved the message.

While waiting for the return call, she returned to the report she received with their case histories and made lists of items needing additional detailed reviews. As far as she could tell, from the files currently available, no items, personal or routine, were missing from any victim. If this was a serial killer, was there some "souvenir" taken, or left, that the on-scene detectives overlooked? She was going to request a list of all items found on or near each victim.

The day passed and Agents Caruso and Woods returned Stella's call as she was shutting now her equipment for the night. She provided them with a brief run down of the situations, and her suspicions. This conversation had all three agents agreeing to meet in Washington, DC in the morning to go over all the details. Stella experienced a sense of relief, knowing that the two agents were going to be involved. She left the office eagerly looking forward to tomorrow morning.

Chapter IX

January 6, 2015
Union Station
Washington, DC

The lozenge bounced twice across the dirty sidewalk before rolling to a stop in the gutter below. "Too much Butter," Sal Caruso grumbled, wiping his fingers on the edge of his heavy wool overcoat. It had the rumpled, slept-in look of a nineteen-forty's pulp fiction detective, not the clean-cut cashmere appearance the Bureau preferred. "…not enough Scotch."

His partner, Steve Woods, had a knowing grin on his face as he shook his head. "I swear to G-d, Sal, those candies are killing you quicker than the cigarettes were."

Sal, a former smoker of some twenty-five years, had fought long and hard to win his battle with cigarettes. The decision to quit came at about the same time he noticed the persistent cough, more like an obstinate tickle in his throat, accompanied with a constant dry mouth.

The first few attempts ended in failure at every Friday night Happy Hour he attended. Then Steve decided that any beer they consumed together would only be drunk as part of a meal in a smoke-free restaurant. As they were both bachelors, and working partners, they shared a lot of meals together. Even knowing that Steve was only trying to help, it did not make the withdrawal any easier. The combination of wanting to rid himself of his nicotine addiction and not wanting to admit failure to his partner carried Sal through the withdrawal process. As of today, Sal proudly acknowledged being smoke-free for every one of the seventeen months, or five hundred and eighteen days, if one was actually counting.

About once a month Sal would stand Steve for a beer at the *Royal Bar and Brewery*, a local pool hall with a fancy name. The Brewery was located a few blocks from their New York City office and was heavily patronized by law enforcement officers, both federal and local municipality. It really helped Sal that the place had gone smoke-free about two years ago. New York City law mandated that change. Now everyone had a new topic to gripe about, smoke-free public buildings, while they drank and played pool. The griping, pro and con, included both former and present smokers.

As an attempt to help squelch any recurring smoking urges, he began using all forms of hard candy...Er, cough drops. To date, his pacifiers have added some twelve pounds to his five foot, nine inch, never-was-slim physique. At forty-nine, with one hundred percent Italian heritage, Sal believed a robust appearance was the natural result of great homemade food, not over indulgence in the candy aisle. No candy in the world could compete with his mother's Cannoli, G-d rest her soul.

"They're *not* candies, for Chris' sake. They're cough drops. For my throat. How many times do I gotta say that? If candy worked, I'd be popping Milky Ways and Snicker Bars."

"Well, if you're going to start that coughing again, you'd better pop something. We're almost there."

Sal thrust his hands deeper into his coat pockets as the winter wind whipped and swirled about. DC, with all its low buildings and open space, always made him a bit uneasy. He had grown up in the crowded concrete tenement section of Manhattan known as Hell's Kitchen, where the pavements were buckled from extensive use and old age and the trash cans on the sidewalks were always overflowing and trash was blowing around. If anyone used a lid for their can, it rarely made it back into the same apartment at the end of the day. One typically fond memory for Sal was that of watching Old Man Thompson navigate his walker around empty bottles as he waddled down Thirty-Fifth Street to the corner liquor store.

Summer time held the strongest memories for Sal. During the nineteen-sixties and nineteen-seventies, for those few months each year, the only thing higher than the tenements was the temperature. The only sound heard above some four hundred window fans or humming air-condition units was the couple downstairs arguing or a radio blasting in the cars driving by. You could smell the sweat, and the exhaust, and maybe the despair of the people that lived there and sweat there and died there.

In Sal's Ninth Avenue world, New York City was bricks and fire escapes and car horns, broken sidewalks and glittering skyscrapers. Washington was different; too short, too clean, too quiet. And, at the moment, too damn cold.

Agent Woods pulled open one of the many main front entrance doors to Union Station, the capitol's bustling train depot. The interior was an odd mix of the old and the new. Roman Sentinels stood midway up to the vaulted ceiling, staring down as neon signs updated the latest arrivals and departures. Shops and restaurants lined the walls, and here and there were scattered long cushioned benches where hollowed eyed travelers sprawled, clutching their luggage.

"There," Sal pointed as Stella's slim figure stood up from a bench in the far corner and waved. "There she is." Steve ran the fingers of one hand through his thinning blond hair as the two agents began to weave their way through the passersby to Stella's location. Despite being somewhere in his mid-forties, Steve still gave off the air of an awkward, gangly teenager, unsure and hesitant at every social encounter.

"Hey guys, thanks for coming so quickly. I was afraid that you might be too buried in another case to get away." Stella flashed them a brilliant smile as they all shook hands. Looking at her watch, and then clasping her hands together, she said, "Almost eleven-thirty, time for lunch. How's pizza sound?"

Sal glanced up at the sign above the fast food mall like restaurant, where a cartoon chef with a handlebar moustache held up a stack of steaming pizza pies. "I don't mind eating here, but its not gonna be pizza. I just know it'll be flat, like that cardboard guy, and it'll be covered with canned tomato sauce and American cheese; all from ingredients prepackaged and shipped in from who-knows-where. No way is that stuff gonna be pizza."

Leaning toward Stella in a confidential manner, Steve told her, "Sal gets a little worked up over Italian food. Maybe we should try the *Buffalo Grill*."

"Or the *Mandarin Chinese Star*. Ain't nobody doesn't like Chinese," Sal added.

Stella and Steve agreed with Sal and after a few minutes they found themselves seated at a small table for four, covered with a crisply pressed white linen tablecloth. Stella sat opposite the two men and placed her overcoat and laptop in the vacant chair.

"So," Stella's face twisted into a mischievous grin, "How is it we agreed to meet at the train station and you guys end up flying down?"

Sal gave his head a shake and looked at his partner, Steve. "See, I told ya she was gonna ask."

"Well," Steve provided, "The flight was cheaper than the train right now. One of the reasons no one questions our expense reports is that we are always looking to save tax dollars."

"You are always looking to save the taxpayers' money," Sal corrected him. "Me? I'm just looking to get the trip over with."

Looking at the two men in front of her, Stella well understood why they made such a great team. They contrasted and complimented each other's actions like a well oiled machine. Not wanting to start the discussion before they had placed their food order, she opted for small talk until the waitress arrived.

"Sal, I'm sure you must hear this question all the time, but, I'm going to ask anyway. With the name Caruso, are you related to the famous singer Caruso?"

Smiling and shaking his head slowly, Sal recanted his familiar tale. "No, no relation. Don't ever name your kid after someone famous. It never works.

Folks in the old neighborhood loved to tell me how they remembered my mother's love of Caruso's voice. I was told that late at night, when the street noise was down, if you stood real still and turned your head toward the sixth floor corner window, the one by the fire escape, you'd hear the scratchy sounds of Enrico Caruso seeping out into the street, the needle swaying up and down as the turntable moved, popping and hissing and sweetening the sound. That would have been my mother, G-d rest her soul, spinning those records over and over, wearing the vinyl out, whispering Enrico Caruso's name to her large round belly. I guess she was hoping I was soaking it up inside there.

I ran as fast and as far from music as I could and I haven't stopped yet. My mother, bless her, passed around twenty years ago, still hoping I'd give up the cops and robbers stuff and try out for the Met. After she was gone, there wasn't anything really tying me to the city. Eight years on the NYPD and I'd seen enough and had enough. I was busting the same heads for the same reasons, and only two things were changing; the age of the perps was going down and the bloodiness was going up.

I applied to the Bureau for two straight years before I made it and I haven't regretted the choice for one minute. I've partnered with Woods here going on four years. He's a quiet guy, which is a good thing because of how much I have to say. And even if Steve may seem kind of strange at times, you know—like spaced out and not quite here on planet Earth?—there's no one smarter, sharper or more dedicated than my partner."

Steve, who had heard the story many times before, always felt humbled by the loyalty and praise Sal showered on him. Of course, he could do without the "strange" reference, even if Sal was talking about his computer skills. Other people didn't know that. As if delivered from heaven, the waitress arrived at this point and Steve was eager to change the subject.

"Gee, thanks for the compliment, I think…Ah, the savior for my hunger pangs has arrived," he commented and smiled at the young bubbly brunette who looked like she was working her way through school. She placed a large pot of hot tea and three Chinese teacups in the center of the table. Then she took out her order pad and pen, posing in a ready position to take their orders. All three glanced back over the menu and each ordered from the lunch combo list. The meals each came with Egg Drop soup and an egg roll. Stella ordered Beef and Broccoli, while Sal ordered Sweet and Sour Pork, and Steve went traditional with Chicken Chow Mein. Smiling at the customers, the waitress left to place their orders.

Stella decided it was time to get down to business. "So, let me review the facts for you," she stated as she pushed two manila folders across the table into their waiting hands. Each folder was filled with dozens of pages of reports.

"We've got deaths in four state capitols. That, I'd say, is way beyond coincidence. Each of these incidents has been treated separately to this point, mostly because of the geographic distance between the sites." Stella paused, and let out a sigh of frustration. "Two deaths I might buy as unrelated, but four definitely implies a link."

"Do you think it's a criminal act?" Steve asked. "I mean, coincidence can work both ways, both for us and against us. Do these state buildings share anything in common? Has the CDC checked the ventilator shafts, the drinking fountains? My first guess would be something along the lines of Legionnaire's Disease, or lead pipe contamination."

"The CDC," Stella informed them, "has only recently entered the picture; since the situation in Georgia. They are playing catch up just like us. I think you guys will need to speak to the coroners at each of the sites. I believe the cause of death in the earlier incidents was listed as heart failure. But, I don't believe heart failure could be so common in all the victims, plus, no one has isolated any instigator for so many cases of heart failure."

Sal's brow furrowed for a moment before he spoke. "Well, that's an awful lot of ground to cover. First thing we'll do is look over all the police activity on the days just prior and shortly after the incidents. I can't count the number of times we've nabbed somebody because they'd gotten a traffic ticket heading away from the scene. We'll go on site, and begin the interview process all over again."

As Stella listened, she couldn't help noticing Agent Woods as he slowly rearranged the silverware, nudging the fork slightly to the left, then repositioning it to the right, also moving the spoon back and forth in front of his teacup. Then he turned his attention to the napkin, creasing and uncreasing the fabric. Rather than appearing inattentive, his face had a stoic expression of deep concentration as he listened to every word his partner spoke.

Steve Woods was a plain brown wrapper man, caught in that purgatory state between youth and old age, between thinness and obesity. He was certainly nondescript, no young girls would sigh longingly as he passed beneath their windows, and no young children would bully their friends for the right to carry his briefcase. He had no noticeable scars, no leg slightly shorter than the other, and his once sandy brown hair, now paling to blond and thinning, was cut in a simple business like manner. He had, since his early teens, a tendency to blend in, to be assimilated, and to be forgotten. At family gatherings, he sometimes wondered if the occasional puzzled look on his parents' faces wasn't a result of them just trying to place exactly where they knew him from. He graduated from high school two years early, and studied Computer Sciences at Berkeley.

He was recruited straight out of school by the Bureau to crack computer firewalls, break codes, and solve numerous analytical issues. Woods jumped at the job, visions of fame and attention foremost in his mind, but he had found himself ignored again. Promotions passed him by, his requests for improved equipment gone unanswered, and he lived his life completely alone.

All that changed a few years ago when he requested regular agent duty, meaning getting out of the computer lab and into the field, and was partnered with Sal. Caruso is his closest personal tie to any form of buddy status. Woods was growing old in the shadows, and feared one day, when he could no longer work the twelve hour days at the Bureau, the world would pass him by completely.

Sal continued to lay out their avenue of attack on the prior situations. "We'll have to begin networking the medical examiners from all the sites, hoping that if they share some information and brainstorm a bit, they can come up with something we can work with. Then, it's on to the victims and their families. We could be looking at a single intended target, and every other dead body might just be there for distraction."

Stella pushed her fingers through her hair, rubbing at her temples. "I'm really worried this thing might just be the beginning. If this is the tip of the iceberg, it's going to shut down state governments across the country."

Steve looked up at that point. "Maybe, Stella, that is exactly the intention, to semi-paralyze local governments. The thirst for control and power comes in all shapes, sizes, and fantasies. I think the *why* of this case is going to be just as intriguing as the *who*."

Their food arrived at that point and all business conversation was suspended for several minutes while the three ate. When Stella saw that the men were now looking at her for continuance, she obliged.

"Okay, let me recap my understanding of this meeting. You two agree that we have a better-than-probable serial killer on our hands. Plus, you have agreed to join me in solving this case." Here she looked at each man waiting for agreement. They both nodded their heads. "I just need to make sure before I formalize our team with your boss and mine. Now, you are going to take the paperwork we have and back track the information, as best as you can." Again a pause for agreement. Again there were nods of concurrence.

"Great, so you two can actually work from your home territory while I remain here. We can use our video teleconference equipment, as well as all our normal telecommunication methods while we do our individual research and analyses. We can always drive, or *fly*," she stated with a twinkled look in Sal's direction, "to any location needing our presence." Both men also agreed with this part of the strategy. Continuing, she told them, "Just to ensure that we have used all possible avenues of information, this afternoon I am going to file a VICAP report, to see if there are any similar historical cases that may help me profile the offender. The Violent Criminal Apprehension Program has been a godsend. The number of criminals that the program has profiled and whose crime sprees have been short circuited is immeasurable."

Sal looked at his watch and saw that they had to hustle if they wanted to catch their return flight. As they stood to leave, he asked Stella where the nearest taxi stand was. Smiling, she told Steve she could help him save some taxpayer money. She then turned her smile on Sal and told him she knew a faster means than a taxi. She walked them to the stairs leading down to the Metro train rail going straight to *Reagan National Airport*. Everyone shook hands, Sal promised daily updates on their research, and the two guys descended down the escalator steps to start their return trip.

    Stella waited until they were out of sight before turning toward the station's entrance, left the building and hailed a taxi for her return to the office. As she settled in the back seat she thought, "Ah, well, what might be good for the goose can really be a bore for this gander."

Chapter X

January 7, 2015
Chairman Von Mumser's Office
Coalition Headquarters
Washington, DC

Richard Von Mumser and Jack Yu, Chairman Mumser's campaign aide, were seated at the twenty person conference table, set in the middle of the opulent office space. The Coalition Committee's Headquarters was located in one of the massive historical buildings lining Massachusetts Avenue, NW. Jack and Richard were going over the agenda for the Chairman's upcoming visit with Connecticut's Governor in two days.

While the itinerary was designed to follow Richard's routine when visiting with state political dignitaries, he always reviewed all the details just before leaving Washington. He believed it was always advantageous to know the latest major concerns and successes in whichever state the visit was to occur. He was most interested in being up-to-date on any issue that he might be able to provide assistance in resolving. This was usually performed with his using his considerable influence in and around Washington, DC. Of course, his ultimate aim was to find a way of ingratiating the Governor he called upon to use his- or-her influence with their congressional representatives in passing the resolution to make Washington, DC the fifty-first state.

Today, Jack appeared a bit distracted while going over the upcoming schedule. Von Mumser watched as Jack thumbed through the pile of papers in front of him, and was, once again, reminded of how much Jack looked like his father did at the same age.

Jack Yu, thirty, had been working for the Chairman since graduating from college. Even before graduating eight years ago, Jack worked as a college intern during school breaks. Jack was an unmitigated believer in the Coalition's efforts for DC statehood. He was also completely devoted to Richard Von Mumser, often displaying idol-worship mannerisms. Richard always felt humbled by the dedication. He was even more elated with Jack's support and enthusiasm for the DC statehood issue.

Richard knew that their initial association was based on Jack's belief that he, Richard Von Mumser, was personally responsible for having saved Jack Sr.'s life from a lethal combat situation during the Gulf War. It was, in fact, a coordinated maneuver by all the soldiers on the scene that day in 1991. But, it seemed, Jack Jr. had bestowed all heroism upon Richard and refused to listen to or accept any other point of view. Richard was the man to whom Jack would be eternally grateful.

As he continued to study Jack's movements, Richard decided to end the suspense. "Okay Jack, out with it. What's on your mind? And don't tell me nothing, because even a blind man could see you are upset about something. We are not going to do another thing until you clear the air. So, spit it out, Jack."

Jack, restacking another pile of papers, stopped in mid-motion and looked up at Richard. The look on his face was one of surprise, as if he were totally amazed that Richard knew him well enough to determine his mood. But then, Jack always looked surprised when Richard correctly read his mood.

Jack saw it as part of his responsibilities to understand and interpret the Chairman's needs and attitudes, not the reverse. His first impulse was to deny any negative thoughts or concerns. Yet, he knew he had to discuss his current doubts about the upcoming trip or he was never going to be able to live with himself. Especially if something went wrong during the pending visit.

"You're right, I am upset. I think you should postpone your trip to Connecticut. At least until the mystery about all these deaths is resolved." Afraid that Richard would cut him off, Jack hurried on.

"Mr. Chairman, if there is some sort of airborne virus, or worse, going around; and something should happen to you, the Coalition would collapse. You are the heart and soul of the committee. Without you, we would cease to exist. That is why I am asking you to please consider rescheduling until these incidents are cleared up."

Not pausing long enough to allow the Chairman to interrupt, he went on, "One major point that bothers me, and should bother you as well, is that whoever is doing this, or causing this to happen, seems to know your schedule very well. Yes, you have made plenty of public appearances without a single negative side effect. But, these deaths seem to have coincided with your trips out of state."

"Jack, I can see that you have given this a lot of thought. But, honestly, what would it look like if I stayed away from someplace, and then nothing was to happen? How can I be a representative for a major issue, having already demonstrated my resolve to stand firm, and bounce back after every defeat; only to start to stay away from places that *might* have a problem? Don't you think that the shadow I seem to have adopted in the form of that reporter from the *DC Daily* wouldn't have a heyday describing the 'yellow streak' running down my back?

No Jack, we have to go to Connecticut, if for no other reason than to show the people of whichever state I am visiting that I am a man of conviction and can be relied upon. Good times and bad. And just so you know, to my way of thinking, with someone out there..." He stopped as he saw the questioning look upon Jack's face.

"Okay, with an *alleged* person out there, doing something, somehow to seemingly healthy individuals; that is what I call a Bad Time scenario. I can only do my best. And if that means demonstrating that I am not only ready to stand for the people, but to stand with the people, I can hardly afford NOT to be there, and in plain sight, right?"

Before Jack could reply, Richard continued, "On the other hand, I really do not think this mysterious someone is actually out to harm me personally. I know you want to know why I can say that. Because, Jack, if someone was really displeased with me, or opposed to something I have or have not done; they would have had any number of opportunities to get at me. It's not like I live my life in a cocoon. There would be no reason to follow me around the country for some form of perceived revenge."

Much as he wanted to find fault with that last statement, Jack could not come up with anything meaningful at the moment. Rather, he reverted to his original argument.

"Mr. Chairman, I still believe that it would be best to alter your schedule just a little. Go a day earlier, or a day later. Just do something different from your posted calendar. Don't you see, that way, just in case someone is aligning their crimes to your schedule, or using your visits to discredit your mission in some way; their plan would fail. You have to see the logic in what I am saying."

Blowing out a puff of air in a manner telling of frustration, Richard looked at Jack, stating, "Jack, if you call me Mr. Chairman, in private, one more time, I will be forced to have to fire you. It's Richard. Yesterday. Today. And Tomorrow. I know that we have had this exact conversation dozen of times before, yet I hope that I have made my point perfectly clear this time?"

To Jack, someone as great and heroic as Richard Von Mumser could never be *just* Richard. This was a man who both served his country during a time of conflict, but selflessly gave of his time and position for all the people of Washington, DC. This man had earned and deserved the respect of being addressed by his title. Yet, Jack also knew how Joe-Average the Chairman saw himself, and wanted to be treated as such. It was clear that in order to move the discussion forward, and hopefully to persuade Von Mumser to see the merit in Jack's point of view, Jack needed to nod his head in agreement. Which he did and then mumbled, "Okay...I promise to call you Richard. But, just as you have said, only in private."

A bit more forcefully, he added, "Will you at least think about my suggestion for altering your short term schedule?"

Richard met Jack's eyes and saw the seriousness there. After all his meticulous research and planning, Richard had no intention of altering his plans. But, he wanted to smooth away any concerns Jack may have.

"Okay, Son, I promise to give your thoughts serious consideration and will get back with you on any changes that may be made. However, our trip to Connecticut starts tomorrow afternoon and really is too short on time for any last minute changes. Should we decide to try any changes, it will have to be for the next visit."

Jack accepted the response and they settled back into his regular pre-trip briefing. Not many hot pockets of discontent were being reported for Connecticut. At least nothing on the national level that might invite the Chairman's involvement. There were a few local issues being debated in the state. But nothing that appeared to require any input by Von Mumser. There was only one item that the Chairman might be able to add some influence with, that of a new building dedicated to famous persons from Connecticut having an impact on the national level.

Connecticut's new Senator was on the new committee for recognition of national citizens of merit and not getting much support from his fellow committee members. Richard was ready to lend a hand and would let Governor Tipa know of his willingness. Of course, assisting others was something Richard relished. And, he did expect those he assisted to also help him, in achieving that elusive goal— Statehood for Washington, DC.

Much against his better judgment, Jack knew the Chairman had made up his mind and there was nothing that was going to stop the upcoming trip from going off as planned. Hopefully, Jack would be able to convince the Chairman to, at least, contain the trip to just the office call with the Governor. Thus canceling the second part of each state visit, that being the Chairman's habit of going into the visitors' area to meet and talk with tourists and local residents.

He understood the Chairman's compulsion, and desire, to make as many people as possible aware of the unequal status bestowed on the citizens of DC, taxpaying Americans without the benefit, protection or privilege of statehood. Jack believed in the Chairman's cause, just not at any risk of any danger to Richard, personally. That was something on which Jack was not willing to compromise on.

Realizing that the meeting was completed, he watched as the Chairman gathered his papers and stood up to leave. As he started for the door, he stopped and turned to say, "Jack, don't forget to get that new order of business cards. Nothing can dissuade a potential supporter more than not having a way to contact us. We can use all the state support we can get."

"Not a problem Mr. Ch…Richard. I will be sure to bring them with the other literature you hand out," Jack replied. *"And I pray you will not be handing them out to anyone"* he added to himself, as he too collected his papers and followed Richard out of the room.

Trailing behind Von Mumser, Jack wondered if another bout of mysterious deaths would be the phenomenon that would sway the Chairman from mixing with so many strangers. Strangers who cannot possibly enhance the Chairman's cause in any way.

CHAPTER XI

January 9, 2015
State Capitol Building
Hartford, Connecticut

Viewing the North Front entrance of the Connecticut State House Building, Richard was duly impressed. The remodeled State House was a mixture of Gothic and French Renaissance Revival. The central circular drum tower, approximately two hundred and fifty-seven feet tall, capped with a gold leafed dome and cupola was an august sight.

As he entered the illustrious building, the monumental spiral stair in the Great Hall moved him. He well understood the Governor's desire to work the majority of in state business from this location. Governor Tipa's office manager welcomed Richard and Jack and they were ushered through security and on to the private entrance for the Governor's working chambers. Jack remained in the hallway while the Chairman went into the private office. After a few minutes of sitting alone, Julius Walsh from the *DC Daily* joined him for the wait.

As Richard entered the Governor's office, Ronald Tipa rose from behind his ornate Cherrywood desk, moving to greet his guest. Reaching out to shake hands, Richard commented, "Ron, so glad you were able to see me today. I know you have a full schedule, including a few state anniversary functions. Thank you for taking this time."

"Dick, it's a good thing that I like you, or this meeting might very well have been canceled. Please, have a seat." Governor Tipa indicated a small seating area against the far wall. There was a floral printed sofa flanked by two end tables facing two plush chairs in the same print separated by a glass in-laid coffee table. The wood paneled wall behind was decorated with numerous awards, certificates, and copies of state historical documents.

"Would you like something to drink?" The governor asked; "Coffee, tea, soda?"

Taking a seat on the sofa, Richard said coffee would be fine. Governor Tipa asked his office assistant to get the beverages, having added coffee for himself. Then, sitting down in one of the chairs, he returned his attention to his visitor.

"Sorry about my earlier comment, Dick. I feel I need to explain myself." Leaning back in his chair, Tipa crossed one leg over the other as he raised one hand and straightened his tie.

Richard both saw and felt the current of unease around the Governor. "Come on Ron, I can see something is bothering you. Out with it. I'm a big boy and I can handle it."

"Okay, I'll admit it; I'm somewhat superstitious about having you here today. It seems that death has been following your travels like a dark shadow recently. I really don't mean to offend you. I know this is not your fault. But, just as an added measure of assurance, for both of our comfort; my security team has been alerted to do full screening of all visitors to the building today. I want to be extra careful that we have a rather unspectacular visit."

Smiling, Richard relaxed, moving back in his seat, "You are not the only one who seems to think that a kook is out there, somewhere, either trying to get at me or to discredit the cause I am trying to achieve. This, by the way, is exactly why I am here."

Not waiting for a reply, Richard launched directly into the one issue that he hoped would get both Ronald's interest on the state level and garner support for the coalition's agenda. "I understand that you may be having a little resistance on your hands getting financial support from Congress for your new national museum to recognize famous natives and residents of Connecticut. Many a Nutmegger has made invaluable contributions to the American way of life and it would be a shame not to have a collective location to acknowledge and celebrate the likes of Ethan Allan, Nathan Hale, Harriet Beecher Stowe, Mark Twain, and Katharine Hepburn, to name just a few."

Richard saw the wistful look of a dreamer cross over Tipa's face. It was mixed with a look of anticipated struggle. Richard took advantage of the moment, "I believe in your efforts and think I might be able to lend some elbow grease to the project. There are several financial investors back in Washington who might be interested in making this a privately funded program. That is, if my conversations with some politicians fail to yield the results you desire. With your approval, it would be my privilege to approach these individuals."

Tipa was listening to every word Von Mumser spoke. He took a few moments to compose his reply. "Dick, without a moment's thought I give you my full concurrence to speak with whomever you think will best endorse this project. I also am not naïve enough to believe that either this visit, or your assistance with this state's program, comes without a price. Am I correct in this reasoning?"

Keeping direct eye contact, Richard nodded in affirmation.

"I also presume that while you ply your political charms in Washington, you wish me to ply mine with our congressional representatives that may have any influence or a vote on the DC statehood legislation. Am I still correct?"

Again, Tipa received the affirmative nod.

While the Governor was pondering the pros and cons of the situation, his assistant returned with the coffee and two pieces of pastry—Nutmeg flavored. As Von Mumser was being served his coffee and Danish, Tipa warmly informed him, "In Connecticut we are nothing, if not always, on the ready to promote our natural resources." Pointing to the pastry on Richard's plate, he added, "In this building, Plain, Sugar Free, and Nutmeg are the only permissible flavors. Want to guess which is the most popular?"

As Richard sipped his coffee, Ronald returned to the previous conversation. "So, let me get this all laid out. You are willing to talk to your associates in Washington on behalf of Connecticut's planned project. In exchange for your help, I will talk to our senators and representatives on behalf of your project. That is the understanding, correct?"

Confirming the Governor's summary, Richard responded, "Ron,

you have always been silver tongued. Yes, that is precisely what I envision. But let me hasten to add. Neither side of our efforts is to be dependent on the success of the other. If my contacts come through for you, the State of Connecticut benefits, period. If your conversations do not materialize into the ultimate goal of my committee, the citizens of the District of Columbia, and I, will continue to march forward in our efforts, period. I am not proposing to offer assistance only contingent on a fruitful conclusion to my campaign. The good Lord alone knows how long we have pursued statehood without success. Does that ease your concerns?"

Richard could see that his comments were right on target as Ronald visibly relaxed in his chair, unfolding his legs and leaning forward in his seat as he listened to every word spoken.

"Yes, actually, I do feel much better about our visit. I can only see an upside as a result of our combined efforts. Again, I apologize regarding my apprehensions about this meeting. It has been most productive, at least, from this Nutmegger's point of view," Tipa concluded with a smile.

When nothing more was said for a few moments, Richard recognized the meeting was drawing to an end. He set down his mug, stood up, and buttoned his suit jacket. Ronald followed suit and the men shook hands. "And now, with your permission Ron, I will go downstairs and mingle awhile with the good citizens of Connecticut."

Tipa's face immediately took on a look of concern, "Dick, do you really think that would be a wise move? I mean, my gut instinct is that you might be safer if you don't make yourself so visible."

Oozing his best charm, Richard stated, "Why, Ronald, your concern warms my heart. You know me. If nothing else, I am a man of habit and dependability. It would serve no purpose, yours, or mine, if I hid away because *maybe* someone *might* have me and me alone, in their cross hairs. Besides, I have learned that there are actually supportive individuals who look forward to my visits. They just want to meet me, shake my hand, and chat a bit. What kind of crusader would I be if I suddenly stopped my public appearances? No, I believe it is the right thing to continue. I hope to do this with your permission."

Still not very comfortable about having Richard out on the main floor, but without a convincing argument to dissuade him, Governor Tipa nodded his concurrence.

With that agreement, the Governor walked the Chairman over to the private office door as they exchanged a final handshake before Richard left the room. Jack Yu and the *DC Daily* reporter, Julius Walsh, were waiting in the hallway. The Governor's assistant accompanied the visitors down to the Great Hall.

Momentarily alone in his office, Ronald Tipa sent up a silent prayer that there would be no deadly trouble on this day.

Surveying the atrium of the Great Hall he was not impressed with the meager display of added security personnel. "It seems that the heralded investigative powers of our law enforcement organizations have been a tad over stated," he told himself. He then thought, "How long was it going to take and how many more citizens were to be sacrificed before they figured out the message?"

His was a brilliant plan, he reasoned, a stroke of genius actually, to deliver his personal message of injustice practically side-by-side with the Coalition Chairman's efforts to garner DC statehood support. With a smirk on his face, he snickered to himself, "Well, we all know how fruitful those meetings have been. NOT."

Objectively he then thought that the manner of campaigning employed by the Coalition Chairman was correct from a political stance. "But, my way will bring the point home faster. The committee's way has proven to be the right thing...always with wrong timing. No, my way is going to be proven the right thing at the right time. When these detectives ever get their act together and reason out why these people have to donate their lives, the Coalition Committee will be eternally grateful to me. I am sure that this strategy will get that statehood issue the attention it needs."

Looking around at all the people in the Great Hall, he thought, "So, who looks like a good volunteer for the cause today?

Sometimes it can be a pain weeding out all the transplants, all those who want to live in a state that they were not born in. But, I must stay with the plan, only native born white men. Maybe I shouldn't have been so restrictive, especially since it seems that women tend to stay closer to their roots than men do. But, I must remain committed and strong, and not vary from the original message. Only white males, period. Okay, time to start the day's process."

It was not unexpected, but still a bit surprising how easily perfect strangers accepted him. Projecting an anticipated political persona, he shook hands with tourists and state visitors at each capitol building. No one seemed to mind when he asked where he or she lived, if they were born in the state or if they chose to live there. No one seemed to notice that he only asked a select few for directions to some local restaurant that he had written on the back of a business card. He told these few that he had heard the eatery was world class and he wanted to try it out while he was in the area.

It was so simple; hand them the card, wait for directions, or acknowledgment that they did not know the location, and retrieve the card. If captured on a security camera, this technique would mirror those campaigning actions of the Chairman and his assistant, Jack Yu; the handing out of literature for DC statehood and a business card. This was almost too easy without a worthy opponent to look beneath the surface.

Everything was going exactly as planned. He had just finished getting directions from the fifth "volunteer" and was in the process of replacing the card in his suit jacket, when someone bumped into his right shoulder. This sudden action caused him to drop both the card and all the other papers he was holding. Regaining his balance, he immediately bent down to retrieve the papers, and primarily the card. He was desperate to get the card before anyone else touched it. His work here today was finished and he did not want to delay his departure nor alter the precise number of volunteers required for this visit, five.

Scrambling to sweep the papers into a pile while scanning the floor for the card, several additional sets of hands entered his view. Passerbys lending a helping hand to recover the scattered papers. He kept his eyes on the floor as he continued to repeat: "That's okay, I've got it. Please, don't bother, I can handle it. See, I'm almost done. Just step back, I'll get everything." Just then, he spotted the card and as he reached for it, a hand came across his vision and picked up the card.

It was not a white hand. It was not a masculine hand. It was a slender tan hand with red nail polish, a gold ring with a ruby stone on the ring finger, and a gold watch on the wrist. The hand with the card moved toward him in an offering manner. The hand was giving the card back to him.

As he took the card, his eyes traveled up the arm to see a very lovely, smooth young woman's face. This black female could not be more than twenty-five years old. It took a few seconds for her words to sink in, "...so sorry. I was in a hurry and honestly did not see you standing there. I really need to learn to watch where I am going. My mother is always telling me to keep my head up. I truly am sorry about the mess."

Watching her expressive face and listening to her talk, he felt the pangs of regret and thought, "Sweetheart, it is too late for you to learn anything more." Aloud he commented, "No problem, don't give it another thought. Thank you for your help. You should listen to your mother." As she looked questioningly at him, he took a few steps back from her, placing the card in his right pocket and added, "Have a good evening."

Turning away from her, he walked across the Great Hall and entered the Men's Room. Once inside, he looked around the room to assure he was alone. He stepped into a stall, removed the card from his pocket, tore it into several small pieces, dropped them into the bowl, and flushed. Moving to a sink, he then washed his hands for a full two minutes before reentering the main hall. As he proceeded to exit the building, several others followed in his wake, to include that reporter from the DC Daily, Julius Walsh.

CHAPTER XII

January 10, 2015
Caption in USA Today's
State-By-State Section

CONNECTICUT: Yesterday, in Hartford, six bodies found in the state capitol building. Five men and one woman. No immediate cause known for the deaths. State authorities are working with the FBI and the CDC. Suspect possible connection with other capitol deaths.

CHAPTER XIII

January 10, 2015
Home of Professor Harvey Cohen
New Haven, Connecticut

"Dad, Dad, did you hear the news? There were some more of those capitol deaths yesterday. And, Dad, you'll never guess! They were right here...in Connecticut." Brandon was talking before he opened the bedroom door.

Harvey was still enjoying the last few moments in a cozy bed before the snooze alarm sounded the second, and final, wake up call. The excited sound of his son's voice had him instantly wide-awake and quickly moving the covers aside. He had his feet on the hardwood floor as Brandon burst into the room.

"Hey, Dad! Did you hear me? It is just too weird, right? Real weird." Brandon was looking excited, not scared, or afraid. Adjusting to the realization that this was not a family emergency, Harvey took the time to look at the clock radio on the nightstand.

"Whoa, Tiger calm down. It's just five minutes after six in the morning. Kind of early for you, isn't it?"

"Yeah, Dad, I know. But, we're having a test in science today and I wanted to go over some facts before school. So, I got up early this morning to study. I was real quiet. I didn't want to make any noise that might wake you up. You didn't hear me, did you? I know Jodie didn't hear me. She's still in her room snoring away." Brandon giggled after making that last statement.

Harvey just looked at his son, and then smiled slightly as he thought how much Jodie hated being told she snores when she slept. Oh yeah, she had tried to use her snoring as justification for a nose job, rationalizing that it would correct her nasal passages and therefore cure her snoring. She was not a happy camper when the ENT doctor said her passages were fine. She just needed some humidity in the bedroom when she slept. He suggested placing a small bowl of water on the nightstand next to her head. Of course, Jodie would not do this and decided that perhaps making noise would eventually get her father to cave in and let her have a new nose. So far her plan had not worked.

What Jodie did not know was that her soft snorts were music to Harvey's ears. He could tell when she was sleeping and not disturbed or interrupted with those recurring nightmares about Laura's accident. After the accident, before the crime scene investigators finished their re-constructive work and had the car towed away, Jodie had insisted on seeing the location.

Harvey had refused to take her, trying to explain that it was important to remember her mother, as she last saw her, not as she was now. Jodie had convinced a couple of her friends to go with her. They biked the two-mile distance to the site. Thank G-d Laura's body had already been removed. But, the car was still there. Jodie broke down when she saw the blood covering the front seats and the lucky charm hanging from the rear view mirror. It was a Star of David that Jodie had made for her mother as a Chanukah gift two years ago. Jodie was so proud when Laura declared it was her lucky charm, put it on a string, and hung it in the car. Now it had become a symbol of death for Jodie. It was months after the accident before she could sleep through the night without nightmares and crying. So, no, the snoring did not bother him at all.

Still looking at his son, he asked, "So, you got up early to go over the test material. That's okay. Now you come running in here with news about more deaths. Is your science test about anatomy? And if it isn't, where did you learn about these deaths while studying?"

Brandon stared at his father as if he just landed here from Mars. "Dad, sometimes you can be so strange. You know I always listen to the radio when I am studying. I'm thinking this situation was on the eleven o'clock news last night cause the radio guy sounded like he was just repeating the stuff. Anyway, how weird is that, Connecticut being the next state to get involved? Wow."

Now, fully awake and on his feet, Harvey pulled on his flannel robe and tied the belt. As he started across the room to the small attached private bathroom, he spoke over his shoulder,

"Bran, I am sorry for all those people and their families. But, if our state had to be involved in with whatever is going on, I am glad that it is over and done with. I will not have to add extra worry or fear to my list if you or Jodie were to go to the capitol on any possible school trips. See you downstairs in about twenty minutes."

Brandon suddenly remembered something out of order with these deaths. Something that was either not noticed before or this was the first time for this situation. He trailed behind his father as he recounted the news item.

"Dad, you remember how all the talk about the bodies discovered before was all men—only men, no children, no women, no nothing else, just men?"

Harvey looked over his shoulder at Brandon, "Yeah, so?"

"Well, this time it was either a way out coincidence or whatever is happening can now effect women. I forgot to tell you. This time they also found the body of one lady."

Harvey turned around to comment, "A lady, you say? Did the report say if she was with one of the dead men? I mean, did it say if she was one of the guys' wife or something? That would be a real shame. Especially if there were any children left behind." He was constantly reminded of his own situation whenever he heard about accidental events.

Brandon took on a look of deep concentration, trying to recall every word of the newscast. "Gee dad, I don't remember anything about that. I only remember the man saying there was one lady. Maybe there will be more about it in the morning paper, or on the morning news. Maybe there will even be some pictures of the people.'"

Ready to change the subject, Harvey said, "Hey Sport, how about a favor. Would you help me out and start the coffee? I know that I only let you have some on weekends, but today is different. We want you to be wide awake for your test. So, make some of that special chocolate flavored coffee, okay?"

That changed the direction of Brandon's thoughts. He loved having coffee with his Dad on Sunday mornings. It made him feel so grown up to have the adult hot drink while they looked through the Sunday paper together. Jodie would tease them when they did this, calling them Oscar and Felix, from the Odd Couple. She watched the show on Nick-at-Nite. Brandon's face lit up with a big smile as he moved to the bedroom door, "Sure…Yeah! That sounds great to me. It'll be ready and waiting for you by the time you come down. Thanks Dad."

A short while later, when Harvey entered the kitchen, Brandon was seated at the kitchen table, arms bent at the elbows, holding his face in his hands, with a very worried look.

"What's with the long face guy? Not worried about the science test, are you?"

Lifting his head and looking up at his father, he answered, "What? Oh, no, I think the science test will be a breeze. I was just thinking. Dad, you don't think these deaths…the ones here in Connecticut are my fault, do you?" He sighed, put his face back into his hands and stared at the table.

That comment was so out of left field, it stopped Harvey in his tracks. "What??? What are you talking about? What do you mean-your fault? How do you figure you had anything to do with this?"

Hurrying across the room, Harvey pulled out a chair and sat down next to his son.

"Brandon, my brilliant, favorite son, look at me," he said as he touched his son's face with one hand and turned Brandon's face in his direction. With his hand still cupping Brandon's cheek, he continued, "Please son, explain to me what brought on that comment. Why in the world, how in the world, could you possibly think that you had anything to do with those tragedies yesterday?"

Anxiously looking at his father, Brandon sighed again, took a deep breath and said, "Because of that talk show a few days ago. You know, the Bubba Meisah program."

Harvey looked mystified. "Yeah, I remember the show. You seemed to have been the only caller who made any comments that the people on the program listened to. That was a good thing, son. Even that lady from the CDC, Ms. Ayin, thought you had a great comment. So, I guess, I'm somewhat confused here, my man. What does that talk show have to do with you or what happened in Hartford yesterday?"

Still looking anxious, Brandon said, "That's just it, Dad. Don't you see? I am the one that got some serious talk from those radio people. Me, Brandon Cohen, from New Haven, Connecticut, Dad. Connecticut, the next state that got hit with those strange deaths."

Then, with a small, childlike voice, he pleadingly continued, "You don't suppose that whoever is doing this was listening and I made them mad and they decided to get back at me, by hurting some of the people in Connecticut, do you?"

Leaning forward and pulling his son into his arms, Harvey consoled him, "No, Son, I do not believe that for even one teeny tiny second. Whoever is doing this, whatever type of sick nutcase it is, has been doing this for some time now. It was just the strangest fluke that Connecticut was the next target. That is what it seemed to be, targets. Your call to that program had nothing at all to do with where this jerk showed up next. Hell, even the police can't find a pattern in what this person is doing or where he will do it next."

Hugging him tighter, Harvey said, "Brandon, you are one very smart guy, and I am so proud to be your father. You have to know that whoever or whatever is taking the lives of these people was doing it before that talk show. And, G-d Forbid may continue doing this until the authorities can figure out what is happening and put a stop to it. No, Son, Connecticut was just a fluke after the talk show. Nothing more. If there is someone, or someone's, plotting out these deaths, for whatever reason, Connecticut was on their radar long before a few days ago. Something that complicated takes a lot of planning."

Seeing that he was getting through to his son, Harvey offered another form of support. With a soft smile on his face, he moved Brandon back into his chair and said, "Tell you what. I have an idea. Just to prove to you that what I am saying is true, why don't you call Ms. Ayin and discuss this with her? Only, you will have to wait until after school. I don't want you to miss the test. But, you can call her office now and leave a message on her machine saying you want to talk with her and you can call back at three o'clock, when you get home from school. How does that sound?"

Brandon seemed very relieved and nodded his head in agreement. "I have her telephone number taped inside my notebook. Can I call her office right now? I mean, I don't want to forget to call before we leave the house."

Keeping the smile on his face, Harvey replied, "Sure, why not. But just for the record, I seriously doubt you would have forgotten to call her a few minutes from now."

He watched as Brandon raced into the den to get the telephone number. Harvey had already made up his mind that he and Ms. Maris Ayin were going to have a parent-to-parent, heart-to-heart chat before Brandon and she talked this afternoon. He wanted to ensure Ms. Ayin did not have any surprise comments that would further upset his son.

Brandon returned with the telephone number and called Ms. Ayin's office. He left the message saying he would call again about three o'clock, and then hung up the phone. While Brandon was talking to Ms. Ayin's recorder, Harvey committed the telephone number to memory. The household returned to a normal routine before everyone left for school and work.

During his first break between classes, Harvey called Maris' office and was able to get through to her on the first try. He told her about Brandon's comments and concerns with the deaths in Hartford. He was gratefully relieved when she replied with much the same conclusions Harvey had already voiced to Brandon. She promised to repeat her convictions when she spoke with Brandon in the afternoon.

CHAPTER XIV

January 10, 2015
FBI Office, Early Morning
Hartford, Connecticut

The Hartford FBI office was on the third floor of the new Twain Federal Complex. The office was accessed through only one entrance, opened by a security guard, after passing through an electronic screening process. Once past the electronic doors, one was met by an office worker who opened the second doorway with a fingered cipher code. Successful passage beyond the second barrier opened up into a large, approximately five thousand square foot office area, subdivided by cushioned cubicle walls. There were five, glass enclosed private offices located at the far end of the room.

"Well, at least there's lots of sunshine coming through the windows", FBI Agent Sal Caruso told his partner, Steve Woods, as they made their way through the maze of office cubicles headed toward the center office, that of the Connecticut FBI Regional Agent-in-Charge. They could see that Stella Vega, FBI Profiler, and their team leader on this case was already in Calvin Jay's office. She either took the first plane out of Reagan National Airport or drove in late last night to be here at seven-thirty in the morning.

They also saw through the office glass the back or side profiles of three other people, two males and one female. The one male in uniform was obviously a local law enforcement official. The female must be their Connecticut counterpart and the second male would the local Chief and Agent-in-Charge, Calvin Jay.

To Sal it seemed that most of the necessary players had already gathered. Minus the six victims, of course. Their bodies had been removed from the capitol building and were now at the city morgue awaiting a CDC representative's presence during the autopsies by state personnel.

There was no need to knock on the office door as they drew near. Stella watched them approach and had the door opened when they were still ten feet away. She waved them inside and closed the door behind them. Once everyone was in the room, Stella made all the introductions. Using her hand to indicate each person, she pointed to her team members first, only wanting to introduce them once. Then she indicated the man behind the desk. "Guys, this is the Hartford Agent-in-Charge, Calvin Jay".

Mr. Jay stood up and shook hands with Sal and Steve. He remained standing as he had been the only person seated. Stella continued speaking, "Mr. Jay is ready to assist in anyway we need. He knows that we are the lead team and he has authorized us full access to all his resources. To this end, he has assigned Ms. Maxine Glenn", indicating the other female in the room, "to work the Connecticut end of our investigation."

Maxine, twenty-five, stood five feet eight inches tall, and weighed about one hundred twenty pounds, looked like she still belonged in high school. Wavy, shoulder length brown hair and wide round hazel eyes completed the youthful innocent appearance. As the agents turned to greet Maxine, Woods wondered how she qualified on the gun range and if she had what it took to actually shoot another human being. Maxine did not shake hands. She smiled, raised her hand, and wiggled her fingers at Caruso and Woods.

"Great, just great", Steve thought, "Agent Jail-Bait just had to have dimples. I'll bet she gets plenty of undercover work at local schools with the controlled substance unit."

Both men nodded their greeting and Steve noticed that Sal even finger waved back.

Stella made the final introduction and the uniformed gentleman was indeed from the local law enforcement. He was Police Lt. John Miller, IV. Approaching fifty, Miller stood five feet, eleven inches, had receding grey/blonde hair and very chocolate brown eyes. He had no problem in the hair department with the bushy silver streaked mustache growing above his upper lip. As he extended his arm to shake hands, Caruso observed that he must have been somewhat of an athlete in his youth. Even though his waist line showed signs of middle age expansion, the rest of him still appeared tight with muscle and minimum fat. Good genes, good gym, or good wife, was what Caruso thought as he took the offered hand and nodded his greeting.

Woods was the social creature in their team. As he shook Miller's hand, Steve commented, "Nice little town you have here Miller. Sorry about the recent mess."

Miller gave Steve a warm smile. "Yeah, I guess to a big bad FBI guy from New York City Hartford might seem like a nice little town. But, we like it and it has enough action to keep my force busy. I'm so comfortable here that I'm even thinking of officially calling this place home."

"Oh?" Woods stated, "How long have you lived in Connecticut?"

With a twinkle in his eye, Miller replied, "Not long, just since I was born, prematurely, at Hartford General. People say I have been in a hurry ever since." Taking on a more serious tone, he added, "I always want to stamp a case CLOSED before the report can be written up. And this case is no exception. Don't know how this psycho got away from my buddies in Georgia, New Jersey, or Pennsylvania, but I have other plans for someone who comes to Connecticut to create mayhem on the citizens. With your help, or without it, this guy is going down."

There were words of agreement from everyone in the room. Stella used this point to refocus the group. "Okay everyone. We all know our purpose in being here. I think the best way to get started is for us to recap what we know, or don't know, about yesterday. So, who wants to go first?"

Jay cleared his throat, drawing Stella's attention, and said, "Agent Vega, I am going to have to leave this meeting in your capable hands. In ten minutes, at eight o'clock, I have a meeting at the Governor's office with the Governor, the Mayor, and Lt. Miller's boss to discuss damage control. As I told you earlier, I, and my staff, stand ready to help in any way needed." Buttoning his suit coat, he moved from behind his desk and walked toward the office door. "Stay as long as you need. My administrative assistant, Mr. Hartley, is seated just outside the office and will get you whatever supplies you need. Sorry for having to leave so soon into our meeting, but some calls cannot be ignored." With that said, he left his office, pulling the door closed behind him.

"Okay," Stella thought, "I guess Mr. Jay is not going to be the first to recap." Looking around at the others, aloud she said "How about you Lt. Miller, what do you know about yesterday?"

Miller took a deep breath and let it out before he started to talk. "First I'll tell you that we have the DC Daily reporter, Julius Walsh, down at our photo lab developing his firm and printing out his digital shots as we speak. Next, we have detained Jack Yu, the aide of that visiting dignitary from DC, Mr. Von Mumser. I figured to hold off on questioning Mr. Yu until after this meeting, it would be best of we only did this once. We don't want any harassment or false arrest charges, do we?"

Stella agreed that the precaution was good. Miller, not finished with his information, continued, "We have also acquired all the videos from the security cameras in the visitors' area and from the entrances into the building. Since we do not have access to any film from the other locations, we cannot tell if there was a repeat face, or faces to be seen. That is, other than the reporter and the aide. But, we have a copy at headquarters that can be viewed for any obvious crimes. Ms. Glenn has the original for your viewing pleasure."

When the focus of attention shifted to Maxine, she spoke for the first time. True to Wood's expectation, she had that youthful voice, not altered by maturity or pollutions. It was a pleasant voice and held everyone's attention.

"Yes, we have the video. I thought we could review it together with tapes from the other capitol buildings. The more eyes the better. We have cordoned off the visitors' area, so no guests today. Lt. Miller's crime scene investigators and ours are still combing the area for any evidence we may have missed during the initial sweep of the location." She looked at Stella for approval. Stella nodded her agreement of the actions and returned her attention to Lt. Miller.

"When you say detained, do you mean you have Mr. Yu in holding, or just not allowing him to leave the area?"

"The latter. Since the two gentlemen, Mr. Walsh included here, are always in the background when Von Mumser goes touring, they are more prime witnesses than prime suspects." Here Miller paused, and then added, "So far."

Since he already had the spot light, Miller continued, "We ran a preliminary background on all the victims from yesterday. Four of the men appear to be upstanding citizens. No trouble with the law that we could find. One man had a restraining order from his ex. Seems the guy is, or was, a drifter, never holding down a job for more than a few months. Always late with his child support, when he did pay and had threatened his ex with physical harm if she reported him. We have already checked, and his ex was at work all day, so no way could she have been here. She works for the school board and was directing a school play yesterday, in honor of our statehood anniversary. Afterwards, there was the usual cookies and juice for the students and parents. She is covered with witnesses."

Miller stopped to take a sip from the coffee cup he held in his left hand. Making a face he said, "Geesh, this stuff is awful. You would think with all our technology, there would be a way to keep hot coffee hot for more than twenty minutes. Anyway, it's the sixth body, the female, Gidget Villareal, which seems so totally out of place with all the recent and previous victims. Ms. Villareal had only recently moved to Connecticut from out of state. From what I can gather, she was a junior member of a local law firm. She transferred here for career enhancement. She was at the capitol yesterday to deliver some papers to the Juvenile Document office. She lived alone, no known boyfriend, not much known about her at all. Her parents are flying in from Iowa and there really isn't much I can tell them. The body cannot be released, pending the autopsy. I have a man at the airport to meet them. I'm thinking, depending on their mental state, to show them the video and see if they recognize anyone. Does that meet with your approval?"

Getting nods from her fellow agents, Stella told Miller that it was a good plan. In fact, she wanted someone from the FBI to be there when the Villareals arrived. She wanted the parents to know that the full force of the law was dedicated to finding the perpetrator. Also, it would be better to have another female there when the parents are told that their daughter's body cannot be released just yet. Stella asked Maxine if she would have someone from the office stand by for the call from Lt. Miller's office when then parents arrived. Maxine said that she would like to do the job, if nobody had any objections. It was agreed that Maxine would work with the parents. It was also agreed that everyone would meet at police headquarters in a few hours to review

Mr. Walsh's pictures from yesterday.

Miller recognized a dismissal and rose to leave the room. As he was pulling the door closed, he paused, stuck his head back into the room and promised them real good hot coffee when they arrived. He smiled and pulled the door shut.

With only the team remaining in the room, Stella asked each one what they saw as a next step. Maxine stated that she had no details yet about the prior cases and she saw herself more in a support position; at least until more information was available. The others agreed with her.

Caruso suggested that they also set up interviews with both Walsh and Yu. Get a view of their character and why each one shadowed Mr. Von Mumser. He suggested that Stella observe their mannerisms and evaluate their honesty, see if they seem to be hiding anything. Also, he wanted Stella to watch their reaction to the security tapes.

Woods acknowledged to himself that he was attracted to Maxine and needed to have her doing something besides being underfoot. He knew that when he was attracted to someone he worked with he became distracted and risked not operating with full concentration. To Stella he said, "I'm sure that Lt. Miller's background checks on the victims were as good as his resources allowed. I suggest that Maxine use our resources to do another check. Then we can compare results to ensure nothing has been overlooked." Looking at Maxine he continued, "I know this may seem like a duplication of effort to you, but it is something we would be doing ourselves anyway."

Glad to be doing something, anything, she totally ignored any condescending tone Woods may have uttered and heartily agreed with the suggestion. She even offered to recheck the victims from the prior locations. Now that suggestion made Steve wince as he and Sal had already performed those background checks. "Say," he thought, "is she patronizing me?" Remembering his belief in having as many eyes look at the information as possible, he told her he would get the names to her.

"Okay guys" Stella said, "now that we have a plan, we don't want to waste any time. So, I'm thinking we should go have breakfast. Then we can visit our colleague, Lt. Miller, on his home territory. Sal, would you call Miller and let him know that we will be there in about an hour? And it might be a good idea if Miller can have the reporter and the chairman's aide available for interviews." Looking around the room at her team, Stella received concurring nods from everyone.

Chapter XV

January 10, 2015
Police Headquarters,
Hartford, Connecticut

As Lt. Miller led the FBI team into the small conference room at Police Headquarters, Stella commented, "Thank you for seeing us so quickly. We brought all our files and the security tapes from the prior capitols effected."

Miller informed her, "Actually, I want to thank you and your agents for your prompt attention to this situation. Agent Caruso said that you wanted to talk with Julius Walsh, the DC reporter and Jack Yu, Chairman Von Mumser's aide. I had a couple of my staff members escort them here. They are waiting in another area of the office, separate rooms, of course."

To clarify, he added, "In fact, Walsh is in the dark room finishing the development of his film from yesterday. Unfortunately any photos he took at prior locations are back in his office at the Daily in Washington. He offered to go get them, but I wanted to wait until you had spoken with him. Walsh appears eager to cooperate. Mr. Yu may be another case."

"Oh?" Stella asked. "Is there a problem with Mr. Yu?"

"Well, not exactly with Mr. Yu", Miller informed her. "Seems his boss, Von Mumser, is not pleased with Yu's detainment. Not pleased at all. Von Mumser is irate that there might be any suspicions cast in the direction of his aide. He said that Yu is a totally honorable, dedicated, forthright individual. He even hinted that we might be singling out Jack Yu because he is Asian and all the victims are Caucasian. We reminded him that Ms. Villareal was neither Asian nor Caucasian, but African American. He backed off a little at that. I got the impression that he was not aware of any female victims. He also insisted on having his personal attorney present when we speak with Mr. Yu. I understand that the lawyer, John Pugh, is in route from Washington and should be here before we are ready to talk with Mr. Yu."

Pausing for a breath, he looked around the oblong eight person conference table, and then added a final comment. "That, pretty much, brings you up to date since we last spoke. So, now, before we begin digging into the details, who's up for that cup of good hot coffee, I promised?"

When everyone accepted the offer, Miller excused himself and left the room to get the drinks. Stella took the time to survey the room. The conference table was placed in the center of the approximately twenty-by-fifteen foot room. The doorway opened into a long hallway that led past some twenty offices, and ended at the other end of the corridor where the elevators were located. Opposite the room entrance was a triple paneled window over looking a main corporate area of Hartford.

Looking back into the room, there were mirrors on both sides of the walls. Smiling slightly, Stella mused to herself, "One real and one two-way? Hmm, I wonder which is which. Does it matter? Nope." A rebellious thought followed, "I would like to know where the microphones are. That way I could make sure that I speak in that direction—for clarity."

The room contained eight chairs spaced around the table. Lining the entrance wall was an office desk with a telephone, computer, and two more chairs. There was a television set with video capability placed on a portable stand. "Everything a good interview office needed," she concluded to herself.

Getting the room ready for the meeting, Sal and Steve placed their paperwork and security tapes on the table. Maxine sat at the end of the table closest to the door, holding a steno pad in her lap, ready to take notes. Knowing that everything they said would probably be recorded; no one spoke until Miller returned with the coffee.

Once everyone was seated, Stella took the lead. "We brought the available background information on the prior victims. Maxine is going to compile the data you gathered on yesterday's casualties with the previous information on the computer database. Then we can search, or eliminate, any common crossovers. I understand that the bodies are still in the morgue. Will they be moved to a CDC location or is an investigator going to come here?"

"An agency examiner is coming here to supervise," Miller informed her. "The thought is that as all the men were local residents, and should there be a need to see, or compare, medical records; here is the best location. Plus, it just seemed kinder to have the bodies here where the families could claim the remains when the autopsies are finished. This seemed to make sense to everyone involved from this end."

Stella's reaction was to agree with the process, "Okay, so let's get started with the information that is available." Looking at Miller, she asked, "If Mr. Walsh is finished developing his photos, would you have him come in?"

Miller nodded in agreement and left the room. A couple of minutes later he returned with Julius Walsh, who insisted on personally carrying his camera equipment, recorder, and the photographs. Miller directed him to the chair at the end of the table closest to the windows. Julius took the seat, but kept his equipment in his lap. Until he knew what this group wanted from him and his photos, he was not going to release anything. He was hoping for a swap of his story for their story. Julius had made copies of all his prints in anticipation of having to part with some, or all, of them. Whenever possible, he liked to be prepared. The worst situation for Julius would be to have a great story, or invaluable evidence, and to have the documentation taken from him.

Stella opened the talk with an effort to ease any apprehension the reporter may have had. "Mr. Walsh, thank you for staying here when your assignment here in Hartford was over. Your cooperation is greatly appreciated." She paused and smiled at Julius, then continued. "My name is Stella Vega and I am with the FBI," here she showed him her badge and identification picture. "With the exception of Lt. Miller, whom you have already met, the others here are also with the Bureau." She then introduced the other agents to Julius.

Stella took the seat to his left and Lt. Miller sat on the right. Before anyone could start talking Julius placed his recorder on the table and told everyone that he wanted to tape the interview for his records, just in case he was able to use the interview, or parts of it, in any future article he wrote relating to this situation. Stella seemed to think about his request and then told him it was okay as long as he cleared any article with her. She explained that in the event there was something identified, either in the conversation, or in the prints, that only the criminal would know, they needed to keep that confidential. "The last thing any of us would want is a copycat killer, right?"

Not one to shy away from questioning others, Julius nodded his agreement, and then snapped on the recorder as he asked, "If you have something that you don't want to see in a newspaper article, does that mean you have a suspect? Is it someone I would know? Has this person given any hint why he, or she, is doing this?"

"Whoa, hold on a minute," Woods told him. "Nobody said anything about a suspect. We just want to be sure that if something **were** discovered, something that only the person doing this would know about, we need to keep that to ourselves. I can tell you that when this case is resolved, we will give you exclusive coverage of any inside details. Does that meet with your expectations and do you agree with our expectations?"

Julius became very excited and rushed to confirm the agreement. "Okay, Agent…Woods, right?" Steve nodded and Julius continued, "Yes, well, Agent Woods, seems we will be working together. I will give you any pictures or information that I have. In exchange, you will share your findings with me. AND, if there is something that must remain unprintable until the case is solved, I will have exclusive interview rights to report the details after the person doing this is caught. Right?"

Steve realized that he needed to be just a tad clearer in their agreement. "Actually, Mr. Walsh, you will indeed have exclusive reporting rights. But, you will not be allowed to report any facts that may not become public knowledge until revealed in a resulting trial. All other information, pending Agent Vega's clearance, will be yours to report as long as your newspaper is interested. We cannot permit anyone, or anything, to compromise this case, or any resulting convictions." Steve paused to let his words have full impact on Julius. "Are you still interested in the deal? I need to know before we proceed or allow the continued recording of this meeting."

While no longer wild about the arrangements, Julius agreed to the conditions. He rationalized that it was a distinct advantage to have inside information that would make his future expose of this case, and there would be one, all the more valuable when he completed the story. He was convinced that someone was trying to destroy Richard Von Mumser's efforts to gain DC statehood. He was also convinced that Von Mumser was going to surface victorious from both his campaign and these shadowing situations at the capitol buildings. And Julius wanted to be the person to pen that piece of history.

Mentally he was envisioning key spots on Investigative Reports and Inside Reporting, two programs centered on his career field. He might even get a big salary hike from this. Dream on, he told himself, not as long as Editor Wellen decided that area of his life. But, there were no road blocks to penning a book. The title could be none other than "Finally—One Nation Under G-d". His daydreaming was short circuited as he heard himself being called back to the present.

"Mr. Walsh? Hello, Earth-to-Julius," Sal was saying. "Looks like you left us there for a minute. Anything you would want to share?"

Somewhat embarrassed, Julius looked down at his recorder on the table and shook his head. "No, nothing significant. I was just picturing the headlines, with my by-line, when this case closes. We journalists have dreams too," he stated as he looked up at Caruso and almost blushed, his cheeks more colorful. Sitting up straighter, he got down to the business of the moment. "I'm sorry folks; exactly what is it I can help you with?"

Sal asked the first question. "How long have you been documenting Mr. Von Mumser's statehood efforts?"

"I cannot be exact on the date when I started, but it has been at least four years."

"Why?" This question came from Steve. "I mean, what makes his efforts so interesting, or important, to you? I understand that you even work off hours if Von Mumser is at a function or on a state tour."

"Well, I guess if anyone can understand an internal obsession to see something completed, it would be you guys." Julius had tried numerous times, with various associates, to explain his compelling desire to be **there** when history was made, with no appreciable understanding. He was hoping for a different reaction from these people. "I'm a reporter and it is my job to cover events and then to convey those events into words, perhaps with accompanying photos, that would have the people reading the article feel like they were there with me."

He looked at Steve and Sal to see if he had their attention, and hopefully, their understanding. They were waiting for him to continue.

A good sign in Julius' mind, so he continued, "However, when I try to explain the feelings I have, that I just have to stay close to Von Mumser, that his burning force is going to be my Pulitzer, I find myself groping for the perfect words to appropriately describe this driving force. Even my boss, Mr. Wellen, is always asking me the same question and I have the same problem when trying to explain my instinct to him."

"I think you explained yourself just fine. I understood your feelings and everything you said." Maxine spoke for the first time since Julius entered the room. "If I may ask a question here?" She looked at Stella, who nodded her okay. Looking back at Julius, Maxine asked, "I understand you may have photos of some of the victims. If so, can you put a name with the shots? That way I can match them with the background data Lt. Miller gave us. It would be helpful if your pictures were listed in the time order you took them, if that is possible."

Julius opened a folder he had placed on the table in front of him. "That is no problem." He pushed the opened folder down the table toward Maxine. "Help yourself to whichever ones you want. I made another set for my records. You will notice that each shot has the date and time printed along the bottom edge."

Maxine smiled, thanked Julius, and started to sift through the folder. Sal and Steve moved to see the prints over her shoulder as she turned each copy. When they got to a print of the lone female victim, Steve reached over and picked up the print. "Ms. Villareal appears to be talking with Mr. Yu. I don't see any shots of her talking with Mr. Von

Mumser. Do you know if the chairman had a chat with her like we have seen him with a few of the other victims yesterday?"

"I can't say for sure", Julius informed Steve. "I was taking shots of the Great Hall and some of the gentlemen, as they queued up to meet the Chairman. All of a sudden there was some sort of loud commotion behind my back. When I turned around, there was the Chairman, Mr. Yu, Ms. Villareal, and three or four other people on their hands and knees picking up strewn papers."

"What happened?" Miller asked.

"Can't say exactly. From what I overheard, it seems Ms. Villareal bumped into someone and papers went flying. As she bent down to retrieve them, she also bumped into another person, with or without papers—I don't know. Anyway, everyone, even some passerbys, got down on the floor and helped gather all the papers for how many ever dropped them. Then a few people just exchanged comments, some shook hands, no one seemed hurt and everyone moved on about their business."

As no one seemed to mind that Maxine had joined in on the questioning, so she asked another question. "Mr. Walsh, from that picture Agent Woods is holding, it would seem that not everyone moved on. Do you happen to know what they were talking about? It might be important if Mr. Yu was the last person to see her alive."

Julius thought about the question for a few seconds, seeming to reach backwards in his memory, as if possible to dredge up that precise moment in time. Then, shaking his head, he replied, "I really did not spend a lot of time on the incident. I just thought it would make for a humorous moment to capture the Chairman on the floor, on his hands and knees. After everyone got up, I just continued to shoot as the crowd broke up. That's the only reason there was even a shot of Mr. Yu with Ms. Villareal. I believed Mr. Yu was just making sure the lady was okay. He's thoughtful that way, always helping out and being kind to people."

Then, as a new thought seemed to come to him, Julius sat up straighter still and said, "Say, wait a sec. If Ms. Villareal was there to deliver a package somewhere in the building, does anyone know who she was to see? Maybe that person was the last one to see her alive."

Not wanting to be left out as they were using his facilities, after all, Lt. Miller spoke up. "Already thought of that. But, she had already delivered her papers and was, in fact, leaving the building. If you recall, from the information we shared earlier today, her's was the one body found outside of the building. Actually, on the steps, where it appears she sat down to rest, not feeling good; something we supposed from the fact she did not call out or draw any attention to herself. So, that brings us back to Mr. Yu as the most likely person to last see her alive."

Julius was stunned to think that Jack might have something to do with these deaths. But, if Jack was involved, maybe there was something he could discover in the pictures he had back at his office. To the group he volunteered one folder of prints, keeping the second folder for himself. He was now eager to get back to Washington, comb through his files and maybe have a story of a different flavor to discuss with his editor. He could already see the headline: "Aide Was Anything But Helpful."

Stella interrupted his latest version of day dreaming, "Mr. Walsh, we have some security tapes from several of the prior state capitol locations. I would greatly appreciate it if you would review the film and let us know if you see anyone you recognize, outside of the official visiting party, at more than one location. Or anything that appears odd to you."

Shrugging his shoulders in a manner to say "Do I have a choice?" Aloud Julius said, "Sure, why not?"

Using the remote control for the video portion of the television, Julius fast forwarded through the tapes until reaching those times that he was in attendance with the Chairman's group. Then he would scan the tapes for anyone or anything that might grab his attention. Unfortunately, the time spent on the security tapes were a waste for Julius and everyone else in the room. He saw nothing unusual.

As Caruso asked the next question, Julius thought he was caught in a round robin version of good cop-bad cop. "Mr. Walsh, we have seen lots of pictures, in fact, almost all of them, are of Mr. Von Mumser. Do you have any pictures of Mr. Yu with any of the victims?"

"I'm sure there have to be some of Mr. Yu. He is Mr. Von Mumser's assistant and an important member of the coalition committee. Pictures of him would be a large part of any story surrounding the Chairman. But, whether any of the shots include any of the victims and Mr. Yu would have to be researched. I can do that as soon as I get back to my office."

Pausing at this point, Julius looked around the room and settled his attention on Stella. "Is there anything else that you need from me at this time? Or is this it? I really do need to get back to DC. I have a story to file, one that everyone in Connecticut has already read about", he mentioned quickly in case anyone in the room thought he was going to rush home to trample the terms of their agreement. "So," Julius added, "I will not be violating any confidences, Ms. Vega. Plus, I have a boss who wants me to earn my salary. Unless there is something else, I would like your permission to leave."

Looking around at her team members and Lt. Miller, Stella saw no objections. "Okay, Mr. Walsh, you can leave. One of us will be in touch with you soon about the other files you have from the other locations affected recently. If you discover anything before we make contact, you will call us right away, okay? I want to thank you again for remaining here and for your cooperation."

Julius nodded his agreement, turned off his recorder, picked up all of his equipment, his folder of prints, and without shaking any hands, quietly left the room.

"Well," Sal stated, "That got us no where. Mr. Walsh seems to have a major case of idol envy where Mr. Von Mumser is concerned. Either that, or, with his eye on his own place in the history. He seems to think he has spotted a potential history making event in that Von Mumser's statehood effort. And, unless he can take pictures and kill people at the same time, he is not going to be a prime suspect."

"Yeah," Steve added, "That doesn't rule out the possibility that he might not have some ulterior motive, and a partner in crime that shadows these functions. Someone he would not "notice" on the survey tapes being at several of the Chairman's trips. Maybe Mr. Yu will be of assistance there."

Stella humorously said, "Hey, are you bucking for my job? Your instincts are right on the money. I do not see or feel that Mr. Walsh is our guy either. He comes across as an eager reporter, with personal fame as his motivator. But, unless he wants that fame so bad that he would create an issue guaranteed to draw national attention, statehood or not, with his by-line; I don't see anything there."

Looking down the table to where Maxine sat, Stella added, "But, just to be totally open in our research; Maxine please add Mr. Walsh and Mr. Yu to your background work." As she looked at her team in general, Stella made a personal observation comment. "It is a sad thing to admit, but I am no longer surprised when a search uncovers unexpected negative incidents about seemingly nice, eager, cooperative people. It does fascinate me how very complex and twisted the human brain can be."

"Speaking of eager and cooperative," Stella said as she looked at Lt. Miller, "Now might be a good time to meet with Mr. Yu. Assuming that his lawyer has arrived."

Chapter XVI

January 10, 2015
Police Headquarters
Hartford, Connecticut

When asked to see if Mr. Yu's lawyer had arrived, Lt. Miller nodded and said he would go check. He left the room and returned within moments. "Yeah, Mr. Pugh has arrived and is with Mr. Yu now. I asked to have them both brought in here."

Five minutes later John Pugh and Jack Yu entered the conference room. Stella rose from the table and walked over to greet the two men. Extending her arm, she first shook Pugh's and then Yu's hand. "Gentlemen, thank you for coming. My name is Stella Vega, FBI Agent," showing them her credentials. Using her hand, she pointed to each person in the room, introducing them as she went along. Finished with the preliminaries, she indicated the chair vacated by Julius Walsh and the one she had been using, "Please, have a seat."

Once everyone sat, and before Stella could say anything more, Mr. Pugh spoke. "Ms. Vega, as you know, I am here at the request of Mr. Von Mumser. My understanding is that his aide here," he stopped and pointed to Jack for emphasis, "and committee assistant, Jack Yu, has been detained in Hartford, without any specific charge being cited. I also understand that this detention may, in some way, be connected with the unfortunate situation yesterday at the State Capitol building. Before I can allow my client to make any comments, I must know the charges being levied against him."

"Actually," Stella informed him, "There are no charges being placed against Mr. Yu at this time. We asked Mr. Yu to remain the Hartford area, more as a possible witness than anything else. As you know, Mr. Pugh, Mr. Yu has traveled extensively with Mr. Von Mumser during the past several years. This would include all those capitol visits where recently unexplained bodies have been discovered."

Pausing to look at Jack and then back to the attorney, Stella continued, "As someone who works mostly in the background, we are hoping that Mr. Yu may have seen something, or someone, that may have appeared suspicious. We have all the pictures taken yesterday by Mr. Walsh, a DC Daily reporter. We also have the security tapes from the Connecticut state capitol Great Hall. We would appreciate having Mr. Yu go through the pictures and to view the tapes with us. If there is someone who has been seen by Mr. Yu at prior locations, or any out-of-the-ordinary situation, we need him to point it out to us. We might also need to ask Mr. Yu some questions. Do either of you have any objection to this?"

Pugh spoke in a whispered voice to Jack for a few moments before responding. "We have no problem with Mr. Yu looking over the pictures or the video. But, it would depend on the nature and direction of your questions, whether Mr. Yu will reply or not. We reserve the right to hear and weight the merit of each inquiry prior to providing a response on record. Agreed?"

Stella appeared to give the typical legal self-protection speech some thought before agreeing to the terms. She knew if anything bad surfaced during the meeting, Lt. Miller would change detained to restrain in a heart beat.

Sal started the session by asking Jack to look through the still shots to see if he saw anyone he recognized, other than the Chairman, from other political events. Jack went through the pictures at a steady pace. He only stopped each time he saw himself in any of the shots. Of the six or so pictures that included Jack, none were with any of the male victims. There were several photos of three of the five male victims, all with Chairman Von Mumser. In those pictures Von Mumser was either talking or shaking hands with the men. Nothing that was unusual or out of order for Von Mumser's normal walk-about when visiting state locations. When the pictures of the victims had been pointed out to

Jack, he did not appear to register any form of surprise or recognition. To him they were just strangers wanting to chat with a national figure or ask for his autograph. Everything in the pictures was within the normal expectation whenever Von Mumser showed up.

When he was finished with the prints, he said that he did not see anyone he knew or had seen at other locations. He mentioned that he knew Julius had been there, and at most of the Chairman's prior engagements; but, with Julius taking the pictures, it would have been hard for him to actually be in any of the shots. "Yes, we thought the same thing," Sal told Jack. Then Sal placed the picture of Jack and Gidget on the table in front of Jack and asked him to explain how he managed to be in a picture with the one dead female from yesterday.

"Wow, is this the lady that died?" Jack asked as he picked up the picture for a closer look. "I had never seen her before. And, until you just told me, I did not know her name. She had fallen on the floor and I helped her up. I just wanted to be sure that she was okay. She said she was, she thanked me for my help, and then she left. That's really all there was to it. I am sorry that she died. She seemed like a real nice young lady." Jack handed the picture back to Sal.

The security tape was viewed next. Jack watched the video with full concentration. Once or twice he asked to have it stopped as he studied a few people. In the end, there was one lady, a reporter for another paper, who Jack had seen at other locations, usually in and around politicians in the DC area. This was the first time he had seen her outside of the Washington area. Jack said that she was probably attaching herself to the Coalition wagon now that there was talk about someone stalking the Chairman or trying to undermine his efforts. But, no, she was not at any of the other locations where bodies were discovered. The other individuals he studied were just look-alikes at first glance, but, upon closer inspection, he dismissed the people.

When asked, Jack agreed to review the other security tapes that were available. Jack explained that the Chairman normally spent about forty-five minutes with the general public. Steve told Jack that they had the security tapes from Philadelphia, New Jersey, and Georgia. No tape was available from Von Mumser's trip to Delaware. The entire process took several hours. During the review of the tapes Lt. Miller sent out for sandwiches and drinks, not wanting to stop the process once they had started. Jack did not ask for any additional stopping of the tapes during the subsequent viewings.

Twice Stella was called out of the meeting. Once for a telephone call from Mr. Jay who asked how the interviews were going and if she needed him to come to Police Head-quarters. She declined his offer, not having anything significant to reveal at the time. The second interruption was to inform her and Lt. Miller that the Villareals had arrived in Hartford.

It was now mid-afternoon and the parents asked to be taken to Gidget's apartment. They had told the police that that is where they wanted to stay while they were in Connecticut. It would help them feel closer to their daughter. Stella called Maxine out of the conference room and sent her to Gidget's apartment to meet and stay with the parents. It was agreed between Stella and Lt. Miller that the interview with the Villareals could be postponed until nine a.m. tomorrow morning. Lt. Miller arranged to have a police cruiser take Maxine to the Villareal apartment.

The viewing of the last security tape was finished at almost five in the evening. Steve asked Jack who the other people were that were handing out paperwork with him and Von Mumser. Jack told him that when the Chairman visited a state location he usually allowed one or two political science students from Howard University and Georgetown to accompany him. The students help to hand out literature on the history of Washington, DC's statehood efforts and the mission of the Coalition. There is one sheet made out with the names of each visited state's Congressmen and Senators, with their websites, mailing addresses, and local headquarter telephone numbers. If the people the students are talking to agree with the committee's efforts that DC should be a state, there is also a form letter provided which they can sign and mail to their representatives requesting a positive vote when the DC statehood legislation is presented before Congress.

The package of material also contains a business card with the telephone numbers and a website address where they can contact either the Coalition Committee or Mr. Von Mumser, himself. The visiting group generally consists of Mr. Von Mumser, one or two rotating spaces for student volunteers, and myself. That is why the faces of our assistants always appear different. The students get credit for internship programs.

Sal asked Jack if he remembered if any of the victims were given the literature package. John Pugh interrupted at this point and wanted to know the purpose of the question. Sal told the lawyer that he wanted to know if Jack himself had given any literature to these people or if Von Mumser handed the literature out or just the interns. Sal stated that he wanted to have a complete understanding of the process. Pugh told Jack that he could respond to the question if he knew the answer.

Jack said that everyone participated in handing out the material. There was no hard and fast procedure for who had which responsibility. "Of course," Jack stated, "because the Chairman did the majority of individual talking, the others in the group did the majority of hand outs. Nothing complicated or unusual. Whoever was closest to the Chairman would either hand a package of material to Von Mumser so he could personally give it to the citizen or one of us would hand it over directly to the person. It is part of our aim to reach as many people as possible, so we moved around the room, not remaining as a tightly gathered group."

Steve asked Jack how he met Mr. Von Mumser. He pointed out that Jack was not a native Washingtonian, like Von Mumser; but rather a citizen of Oregon. So, why was he, Jack Yu, a part of Richard Von Mumser's Coalition Committee, and actually, Von Mumser's personal assistant. "Do you believe in your boss's ultimate aim?" Steve asked. "Or, is there another reason for your dedication? Do you have political ambitions of you own? I mean, if Von Mumser is successful in acquiring statehood for DC while you are his main aide, is it possible that other people may credit Von Mumser's accomplishment to your efforts and make you financial offers to assist them on other projects?"

Mr. Pugh had been sitting back in his chair, but those questions had him sitting up straight in his chair, placing his forearms on the table. "Jack, don't answer those questions yet." To Steve he asked, "What is the meaning of those questions? What are you trying to imply? Are you hinting that Jack is not a dedicated, honorable person? That he is working with Richard Von Mumser for fame and fortune? This, by the way, is what a lot of people do when they pursue working knowledge and experience in their chosen profession."

Taking on a harsher tone, he reversed the line of questioning on Steve, "I might ask the same question of you, Agent Woods. Why do you work for the FBI? It is highly unlikely that you are doing it for the money. But, maybe you have ambitions to work your way up the ladder to regional director or maybe even the number one spot. Are you in law enforcement because you have a fame and power issue?"

Steve was well acquainted with lawyers attempting to change the direction of questioning by implying that the law officer was after some type of special attention or acknowledgement when questioning their clients. He was not about to indulge Mr. Pugh in his attempts at diversion. "Mr. Pugh, my employment is neither the issue nor the purpose of this interview. However, Mr. Yu's employment desires are and I would appreciate an answer."

Jack put his hand on Pugh's forearm. "It's okay John. I really don't mind. I have nothing to hide and really would like to answer Agent Woods' questions. It's okay, really." Pugh looked at his client, nodded once and sat back in his chair placing his elbows on the chair arms and interlocked his fingers, then placed them under his chin.

Jack looked around the table at everyone then spoke directly to Steve. "Whether I believe in statehood for the District, or not, is not why I have chosen to work for and be associated with Richard Von Mumser. Yes, I said that I have chosen to work with him rather than he having selected me.

To me, Richard Von Mumser is a hero in the purest sense. My father was stationed in Kuwait during the Gulf War at the same time as Mr. Von Mumser, then Major Von Mumser with the DC National Guard. One day my father's unit found themselves surrounded by the Iraqi National Guard and about to be annihilated. Mr. Von Mumser, I mean, Major Von Mumser, like the fabled cavalry of old, came riding to the rescue with his unit and, basically, saved the day. They were able to subdue the enemy and free the American soldiers, my father being one of them. To my way of thinking, that makes the Chairman a hero, regardless of how he tries to downplay his actions that day."

Jack stopped to take a swallow of water from one of the bottles Lt. Miller had placed on the table when they arrived and then continued, "As to having any personal political ambitions…Yes, I do have them. But, only as far as remaining in a circle of politics and influence connected with the Chairman. Because, when he is successful in his campaign to see DC obtain statehood, and he will succeed; there will be other projects that will require his time and talents, not mine. And he will still need a chief assistant. That is where I see myself. That is where my ambition lies. I hope that answers your questions."

"Yes, thank you that does answer those questions." Steve replied. "Now tell me, Mr. Yu, do you know of anyone, for any reason, that would be happier with Mr. Von Mumser's failure than with his success?"

Immediately Pugh was in action mode again. "Jack, that question you definitely do not have to answer. It would only be speculation on your part." Turning to face Steve, Pugh continued, "Any enemies that Richard Von Mumser may, or may not, have can be provided by a talk between your agents and Mr. Von Mumser himself." Jack looked first at the lawyer and then at Steve, all the while with a very uncomfortable expression on his face.

"What is it Mr. Yu?" Steve inquired, "I can see that something is troubling you."

"Jack," Pugh interrupted, "this is not your concern. I'm telling you to leave things alone."

Ignoring the attorney, Steve again urged Jack to speak. "Mr. Yu, if you know something that can help us, or may even save someone's life, you have a civic responsibility to speak up."

Jack settled his attention on Pugh and spoke, "It's not like I would be revealing anything that everyone doesn't already know. Don't you think it would be kinder for us to tell the authorities than for them to question the Chairman and bring up painful memories?"

Pugh recognized that Jack was going to tell the Agents about a family situation that he, John, did not agree with disclosing. While it might be easier on his friend if Jack did reveal a family blemish, he did not want to witness the telling. Rather than acknowledge Jack's comment, Pugh looked at Lt. Miller and asked to be excused for a few minutes. Miller understood Pugh's action; to be able to honestly tell Von Mumser that he did not know what, if anything, negative was told to any law officer. Miller agreed to Pugh's request.

Once Pugh had left the room, Sal asked Jack what was it that he wanted to say. Jack insisted that he wanted everyone to understand that he did not personally know of anyone that could be classified as an enemy. The people that he had met during his association with the Chairman had only positive statements about Von Mumser. That even included those that did not support his campaign.

"Okay, okay," Caruso said, "I see what a paragon of virtue the man is. So what is it that had you looking like you just swallowed sour milk a few minutes ago?"

"I'm getting there." Jack replied. "I just wanted you to know that the Chairman does not have any enemies." He paused a few seconds, seeming to think on how best to present his information. "You should know that while the Chairman has great rapport with just about everyone, there is one person who would rather have nothing to do with him. I don't think that this person dislikes him enough to cause the Chairman any harm, he would just rather have no contact with him."

When Jack did not provide any further information, Woods asked the obvious question. "And that person would be?"

"His son…. Josh," Jack supplied and seemed relieved after making the opening statement. Rapidly he continued, "I cannot remember the last time I personally saw Josh in his father's company. But, from the bits and pieces of conversations I have heard over the years, the Chairman and his son do not get along. In fact, they have not been in the same room for many years. Josh comes to visit his mother only when the Chairman is away. And Mrs. Von Mumser will visit Josh and his family only by herself. Josh seems to be a subject that Mr. and Mrs. Von Mumser avoid like the plague."

"And where is Josh now? Where does he live? What does he do? Do you know how to get in touch with him? Better yet, do you know how we can contact him?" Caruso rapid fired the questions.

Jack sat back in his chair, as if moving away from physical punches. "Hey, not a problem, okay? Just slow down a bit, okay? Josh lives in Arlington, Virginia. He is CEO of a Pharmaceutical firm that has its headquarters in Vienna, Virginia. I personally do not think it would be appropriate for me to call Josh. Seeing as how we have not actually spoken to each other for years and he knows how much I respect his father. I can give you the information and you can call him yourself, if you like."

"What makes you say that it would be inappropriate for you to make contact with Josh?" Steve asked.

"Well, the last time we actually spoke, Josh told me to only call him if his father were dead—but not for any other reason. So, I guess that pretty much said it all."

"Not exactly," Miller said, "What caused this rift….according to those pits and pieces you have heard?"

"I have put together that Josh blames his father for his mother's nervous breakdown years ago. It seems that Josh believes that his father's driving obsession for DC statehood occupied the Chairman so much that he either ignored his family in the process or took out his frustration on them. That had Mrs. Von Mumser turning to drugs to cope with her life. That eventually led to her breakdown. Whether those accusations are true or not, Mrs. Von Mumser's condition seemed to cause a turnaround in Mr. Von Mumser's attitude toward his family. While it appears to have been too late to mend the differences with his son, he and his wife have never been closer. Mr. Von Mumser truly loves his family and, it seems, had to almost lose his wife to realize the pressure he was putting on her. Josh has never forgiven his father. Or, at least that is what I have gleaned."

At this point Pugh knocked on the door and asked if it was okay to come back in. Miller told him to come in. Pugh entered and looked around the room. He asked if everything was okay. When Steve informed him that there were no more questions for Mr. Yu at this time, Pugh and Jack got up to leave the conference room. Before Jack left the room he spoke to Stella telling her that he would make himself available, if needed, at any future time. He even volunteered to review any additional pictures Mr. Walsh may present to her. Jack continued to address only Stella when he said his goodbyes, giving her his business card with his personal cell phone number hand written on the back. He told her she could call him at any time. Stella thanked him and returned the gesture by giving him her business card, without any personal cell phone number.

When the agents and Miller were alone in the room, Stella announced that the most interesting new lead that they got was that relating to Von Mumser's son. She admitted it had been a very long day and no more could be done at this point. She asked Lt. Miller if he would accompany the Villareals and Maxine in the morning when they viewed the security tape. He agreed to the request and said he would provide her with a follow up report of the meeting. She then told Woods and Caruso to follow up on the lead concerning Josh Von Mumser. They were to contact the man tomorrow, have a talk with him about the alleged rift in the family and to do a background check on him. Especially on his recent activities, see if he has been away from his business on any dates that coincide with Von Mumser's trips.

As they gathered their papers, prints and tapes, Stella told them she was going to call her CDC contact tomorrow to see if there was anything new from the autopsies or the toxicologist.

With the settlement of new assignments, Miller suggested that maybe the agents would like to join him for dinner at a local restaurant that served world class steaks. Everyone thought that was a superb idea and agreed to meet at the steakhouse at eight o'clock.

Chapter XVII

January 11, 2015
Stella Vega's Office
FBI Building
Washington, DC

The day was starting out as uneventful as yesterday ended. Maxine called at eleven a.m. to report in about the Villareals review of the photographs and security tapes. If Gidget knew anyone that had been captured on celluloid, the parents did not know them. In a word, Nada. Nothing was learned from the meeting. The Villareals did want to know when Gidget would be released so they could take her home for burial. The parents had given the FBI full authority to search their daughter's apartment if it would help solve the murder.

Maxine told Stella that the parents insisted on staying in Gidget's apartment until they left town. Mrs. Villareal wanted to go through the apartment, sorting out what needed to be packed, left behind or given away. Maxine related the parents' desire that everything be finished before they left the state. They did not want to come back to Connecticut again.

Stella told Maxine that she would have to call her back on the release of the daughter's remains. She was going to contact the CDC Regional Superintendent and would ask the question.

After the phone conversation with Maxine, Stella did as she said she would and placed a call to Maris Ayin. As soon as Stella heard Maris' voice she felt a sense of comfort. Maris never seemed frazzled and always spoke in a calm voice.

"Maris, Stella here," she said as she spoke in the direction of the open speaker on her office telephone.

"Maris, this is Stella. Thought I would give you a couple of days to digest the details from the latest set of victims. Have you got anything that you can share?" Maris asked her to hold a few moments while she got her papers.

Stella was seated at her desk with five stacks of folders spaced across the top. Each stack was labeled with a state's name; Delaware, Pennsylvania, New Jersey, Georgia, and Connecticut. She had a steno pad in front of her and a pen in her left hand, ready for taking notes. Looking at the pen she had a flash back to her childhood when she was first learning to print letters on paper.

She had been worried that she was a strange person because all the other children were using their right hands to print. When she tried using her right hand it felt like she was trying to move a very heavy object and her fingers did not want to cooperate in letting her hold the big pencil in the same easy way that her left fingers worked.

She remembered thinking that the fingers on her right hand must be broken or that G-d was angry with her for some reason and would not let her be like all of her classmates. The teacher did not see anything wrong with Stella using her left hand. Then, when she got home she cried as she told her mother that she did not want to go back to school and be different.

Her Mom, bless her, patiently listened to the five-year-old's tale of woe. Then she smiled, hugged Stella, and told her that people who wrote with their left hand were special, not strange. Her mother explained that only a few people were able to write left handed and that it took more brain power to master using the left hand. So, if, right from the beginning of her education she showed she had more brain power than the other children, she had to be special and chosen to do wonderful things with her life. But, her Mom told her, she had to really be careful with her brain power and not tease the other students. Stella remembered going back to school full of confidence and pleasure in having a secret that she shared only with her mother.

She was pulled out of the past when Maris came back on the line. "Sorry for the delay. It was my plan to call you sometime today. Seems great minds do think alike."

Stella was tempted to ask Maris if she was left handed. But instead replied, "Okay, ye of the great-mind-society tell me great things. Or, at least one great thing that will help me to formulate a reasonable profile of this character with a fetish for state capitols."

"Oh, is that part of the profile, Stella? A desire to litter the hallowed halls with homicides?"

"Actually, Maris, I have been thinking about what type of person is behind this. Obviously, the capitol buildings hold some special meaning to him. I just haven't been able to put my finger on it yet. But I have faith, it will come to me. So, my friend, now it is your turn...tell Stella all."

Maris was warmed by the friendly tone in Stella's voice. Yet she knew it was time to return to business. She also knew Stella was not going to be happy with her current analyses. "I have done an extensive review of all the autopsies on all the victims from Delaware to Connecticut. Of course my staff is going to research additional toxicology analyses. I have sent people to each location and hope to have something to report soon."

"With the exception of the one female, all the bodies were those of while males. They ranged in age from twenty-three to sixty-seven. They also ranged from top physical condition to a few with ulcers, high cholesterol, high blood pressure, one case of advanced cancer and one case of HIV positive. This we know from the bodies and the prescription medications in their systems or on their person. All make and manner of human beings. The one solitary common denominator is the manner of death. They all, including the female, expired from a total shutdown of their internal systems. My preliminary conclusion is death by poison, or poisons, unknown.

We also cannot provide or develop an antidote until we know what we are dealing with. Sorry Stella, I know this is not what you wanted to hear. But, we have narrowed the field of possibilities by a measurable amount. We just need to find that elusive chemical and we will know what we are dealing with. We will also know if there is an antidote, if administered quickly enough, to stop the shutdown. I have tasked a few ace researchers to begin searching all available files for known toxins with the properties, or near properties, that would resemble our victims.

It may take a few days. I promise to contact you as soon as I have some-thing to report." They exchanged expected farewell comments and disconnected.

Stella had been hoping for a more definitive report, but was pleased with the new information. Now they just had to narrow the field to who and how. But then, she thought, the who and how was almost always the easy part. After that, the suspect only had to provide the FBI with an opportunity to catch them. Just the knowing was not enough. In fact, having too much information about a crime and a potential suspect could be more frustrating than not having enough data.

It seemed that most prime suspects, who later proved to be the actual perpetrators, always thought they were too clever to be caught. Of course, ninety-eight percent of the time, justice prevailed and the extra time spent tracking the "clever" criminals made for good experience. But it clearly put a drain on the constrained Bureau resources.

So, she thought, here we go again; another clever guy who is thinking he is not going to be caught. Someone who is either infecting these people before they enter the buildings, or, somehow, is able to infect them without raising any suspicions. That thought had her making a note to check for any security cameras out-side the buildings. It was worth the effort to see if anything was available that may have been over looked.

She now made a few more notes, more as food-for-thought notes than as actual pieces of evidence.

—Was this someone who does not raise suspicion?

—Was this person too far below the radar? Like?? Building security? Building maintenance? Food handlers? Tour guides?

—Or, too far above the radar?

Like?? The Governor? Aide to the Governor? Politician? Aide to politicians? Head of security?

—Discuss with team!!!!

Putting down her pen, she closed her eyes and let her profiler instincts take over. Those instincts told her she was looking for an "above the line" person. Unless, there was a very disgruntled chemical genius working "below the radar"? Someone who was going state-to-state for each situation and successfully passing background checked and gaining employment in time for another death spree? Nope, unless that scenario popped up, "below the radar" was going to prove useless. Still it was a check that had to be done. She was going to suggest that either Steve or Sal task Maxine to review the employment records with special attention for any potential job drifter.

With that task formed in her mind, she turned her thoughts to the "above the radar" probabilities. She felt the person they were looking for was most probably a male. Someone with knowledge of either medicine or chemistry. Perhaps someone like Richard Von Mumser's son? But, if it is Josh Von Mumser, no one seemed to notice him at any of the crime scenes. Maybe that's because he never came into the buildings? We definitely need to find out if there are any outside cameras. However, if it is the son, and he has alibis for the dates of the crimes, maybe he could have hired someone? She was eager to have Steve or Sal report in on their meeting with Josh Von Mumser and if they were able to learn anything. But, if not the son, then who else would be at all the sites? She knew they were already doing backgrounds on the reporter and the Chairman's aide. And, as she had learned from Jack, the committee interns were on a college rotational basis. Still, she wanted a list of the students' names to insure there were no repeat volunteers.

As she sat and let the feelings flow, she also felt that they were looking for a Caucasian. She was being as open in her thoughts as possible. While America may have come a long way in racial equality since the shameful days of slavery, white people still did not flock around prominent non-Hollywood persons of color. It did not matter if that person was brown, black, yellow, or red, white did not rush to embrace them.

Stella reasoned that the lone black female was either a random copy-cat killing, or a definite target of a separate case, or just a true fluke of being in the wrong place at the wrong time; a mistake, or a deliberate diversion. No, she thought, Gidget Villareal needed to be removed from the serial victims.

It was the white males that were the main point here. She knew she was missing a vital clue that somehow connected all these men. Something that would scream **obvious** when she saw it. It remained outside her reach at the moment.

Reasoning, experience and knowledge allowed Stella to determine that the crimes were not nearly as random as they appeared. Yes, the crime dates had no discernable intervals. Yes, the crime scenes varied. And, yes, other than being white males, the crime victims' lifestyles were as different as a populace could have. She needed to find the path that would connect the dots.

The victims themselves may actually have been the only random piece in this case. It was way too far outside the range of probability that could arrange to have each victim at exactly the right location, at exactly the precise time, on some unknown date. No, it was pure chance; unfortunate as it was that had each man at a state capitol when tragedy struck. So, random occurrence was definitely not a possibility for the site selection. Yet, random occurrence was the selection process for the victims.

She opened her mind further to the visualization of the person they could be looking for. The strongest impression was of a white male, forty-five to sixty years of age. He would be average height, able to look most other men eye-to-eye. He possessed an air of charisma, able to make people feel comfortable in his presence. He would be someone people could approach, trustworthy, not someone people would shy away from or recall for being different.

He would be educated, possibly with a Masters, or a Ph.D. And, he would have good communication skills. He either felt he was smarter than the law or was challenging the law to discover him. The sixty-four thousand dollar question remained: Why?

Her thoughts took another turn, away from the profile of the killings and towards a possible motive. What was the message he was sending? Why these men? What made them the targets?

Her thoughts then turned again to the only link she knew that ran throughout all the known locations: Chairman Richard Von Mumser. A visiting dignitary at each site on each date. Was someone using his statehood campaign as a cover for a personal agenda? Was someone trying to discredit Von Mumser's objective? Did someone have an old grudge or vendetta against Von Mumser? Or against the District of Columbia? Or, was someone actually after Von Mumser and was playing some sick game of cat-and-mouse until the real target was eliminated?

"Damn," she said out loud, "Questions, questions, and more questions, but no answers. I want answers. And the sooner the better, before more lives are lost." Taking a deep breath to refocus, she wondered when she was going to hear form Steve or Sal. As if conjured up by magic, her desk phone rang. When she answered, it was Sal. He was checking in with an update on their trip to see Von Mumser's son.

"Sorry Boss Lady, but we ran into a brick wall. Seems Mr. Josh Von Mumser, and family, are out of town. In fact, they have been on vacation for the past week. Someplace warm is all I could get out of the Gargoyle who guards his office. Our badges had no effect either. Said she wanted to see a search warrant, which we did not have. But we can get one and go back. Oh, yeah, Dragon Lady said Josh is due back at the office in three days. Your call, Boss."

Stella agreed that an open search warrant was a good idea. That would allow them to serve the warrant at any location. But she saw no rush to go back to Josh Von Mumser's business at this time. Meeting the son could wait a few days. It would allow them ample time to do a good background check on the man. She told Sal to get back to her as soon as they had something.

Chapter XVIII

January 12, 2015
DC Daily Newspaper
Editor's Office
Washington, DC

 Editor Don Wellen sat at his desk drumming his fingers against the top surface. Being the patient soul that he wasn't, he did not know what was taking his reporter, Julius Walsh, so long to get to his office. He had had Julius paged fifteen minutes ago. Wait, he told himself, those were footsteps and voices approaching the office. Of course whoever was approaching was doing so from the side of his glass fish bowl office that actually had a solid wall.
 Before he could pretend that he was his usual busy self with late breaking editorial page business, the door to his office opened, without a knock, and in strolled Julius Walsh and an intern reporter from Howard University, who was carrying several nylon folders in his hands. Julius ceased his talking with the intern, faced his boss, and asked, "You wanted to see me Boss?"
 Wellen stopped the finger concert and placed both hands, palms down, on the desk as he pushed himself out of his chair to face Julius eye-to-eye. "Well, well, the prodigal reporter comes home. You're darn right I want to see you. But, more to the point, I would think you would want to see me. To tell me you have some exclusive photos of the latest victims; to tell me that you saw something suspicious with those blood hound reporter instincts; to tell me you may even have a suspect we could let the police know about. So, now tell me I'm right, Mr. Walsh."
 "Okay, Boss. In answer to your areas of concern I can say; Yes to the first, No to the second, and Maybe to the third."

Wellen visibly relaxed and sat back down in this chair. "Alright, now we're getting somewhere. I think we need to take this one step at a time. First, the pictures. What have you got?"

Taking the folders from the intern, Julius placed them in a stack on the Editor's desk. "Sir, I have gone through all the pictures I have taken since documenting Richard Von Mumser's Statehood campaign." When Wellen made to reach for the folders Julius stopped him. These pictures were his babies and he did not want anyone, even his boss getting them mixed up.

"Wait Boss. Before you start going through all the pictures, and possibly getting them mixed up, I need to tell you what is in each folder. The folders are numbered. In Number One are the photos and articles surrounding political functions that Von Mumser has attended. In Number Two are the photos and articles relating to the Coalition Committee events. In Number Three are photos and articles from Von Mumser's state trips, to include the last five trips of interest. But, I believe that the folder you will want to see is Number Four. In that folder I have isolated all the photos of possible interest from Von Mumser's trips to Delaware up to two days ago."

Wellen was surprised at the amount of prints in each folder. Well, this helped to explain Julius' expense account. Wellen put out his hand and Julius handed him the fourth folder. While Wellen flipped through the prints, Julius continued to talk. "As you can see, the majority of the prints are either of Von Mumser or Jack. The other people in the photos with them are known victims. There are also a few shots of just strangers that turned out to be victims, including the lone female from Connecticut. I have put stickies on the back of the prints to explain who each person is. You will notice a few individuals that show repeated appearances. They are statehood supporters and no one person attended all the events. At least, I did not see anyone suspicious appearing at all the events."

"So, I guess that would be the No to my second area of concern, huh, Walsh?"

"Yes sir, I'm afraid it is."

"Well," Wellen went on, "you said that you had a maybe to my third area of concern. Let me have it."

"Yes, well, actually, I don't have any suspect, but I believe that the FBI thinks that perhaps Jack Yu may be a "person of interest", was how they put it. I, personally, do not see Jack as anyone who would hurt a fly. Besides, he practically eats, sleeps, and drinks at the altar of Richard Von Mumser. The guy is a real idol worshipper. But, here is the best part, Boss. While I was being questioned by the FBI in Hartford, we struck a deal."

"Deal? What kind of deal?" Wellen asked.

"Actually, a great deal for us. They wanted to use some of my prints and videos of the victims and surrounding crowds. In exchange for my cooperation, they have promised us exclusive coverage of any developing information in this case. The only issue with the deal was that if we come up with some-thing that may be a potential piece of evidence in a trial, that we need the FBI approval before we print it. Or, we may even have to hold the information until an arrest has been made."

"Okay, that sounds reasonable to me. But, I have to tell you Kid, if you have something really big and other papers have some of the same info, and they are going to go to press with it before us, I may have to countermand your agreement with the Feds. Understand? If something is going to become public knowledge, then it needs to come from the Daily first."

Julius just nodded at his boss's comment. He really wanted to stay on the story and the inside track with the FBI.

"Got any other thoughts on this case?" Wellen asked.

"Sort of. I was wondering if maybe someone on the coalition committee is jealous of Von Mumser's influence and attention. Maybe there is someone on the committee who wants to throw dirt or doubt in his way."

"Sounds like a hunch. Check it out." His boss directed.

"Also, Boss, I learned that the CDC has not been able to identify the exact cause of the deaths. The CDC knows that it was some type of chemical, but the exact poison has yet to be identified. Agent Woods of the FBI told me that I would know that information as soon as they do. Of course, that may be something that we have to hold onto until an arrest occurs."

"Okay, I can see the advantage of keeping your agreement with the FBI. Not that I am enamored of the deal. I want you to stay on the trail of your theories. And you should tell the FBI about the statehood supporters that you saw at several of the state visits. Also, maybe you should pay a visit to Jack Yu and show him the same prints and see what he has to say."

"Yes sir, I can do that this afternoon. As soon as I return these prints to my office. I certainly don't want to misplace any of these."

"Kid, I think you are finally developing that blood hound instinct we've been talking about. Now I want you to stay in Von Mumser's back pocket and see what you can uncover."

"Can do. Yes sir, can do." Julius said as he picked up the first three of the four folders, leaving the last with Wellen.

As he was about to leave the office Wellen commented, "I have to admit something. I've been thinking you were just wasting your time trailing around behind Von Mumser and his objective that has eluded the District of Columbia for centuries. But, maybe, you have fallen into a real story with teeth. Good luck, Kid." Julius nodded and left the office.

Chapter XIX

January 14, 2015
Josh Von Mumser's Office
Von Mumser Pharmaceuticals
Vienna, Virginia

When Sal and Steve stepped off the eleventh floor elevator into the plush reception area, they were immediately met by The Dragon Lady from three days ago. "I'm sorry but Mr. Von Mumser has just returned to work and has appointments back-to-back all day. I can schedule you for an appointment time, if you need to speak with him."

While Steve reached inside his overcoat to withdraw their search warrant, Sal presented the executive secretary with his most charming smile. "And when would you be able to squeeze us into your boss's busy schedule?"

Dragon Lady looked down at her appointment calendar, and then informed them that the first possible opening was not for another two days. And, she added, that would only be possible for fifteen minutes.

Steve presented her with the warrant and said, "Well, I think Mr. Von Mumser will see us—Now." Looking around the reception area, he counted five doorways into private offices. All the doors were closed. "Would you be so kind as to point out the doors for Mr. Von Mumser's office?"

Dragon Lady hesitated. "Mr. Von Mumser is holding a meeting right now and he does not like to be interrupted. I will have to go inside to let him know you are here."

"Oh, don't bother," Steve told her. "We're real good at introducing ourselves. Just point out the correct entrance." When she still did not move, Steve lost some of his normal cool. "Now lady or I will be forced to charge you with obstruction of justice." When Steve said this, Sal smiled even more and thought to himself, "Oh, please, don't move and let me be the one. I would love to have the privilege of teaching this broad that you really do catch more flies with honey than vinegar."

Dragon Lady looked at Steve as if she could envision him on a slow spit over a roaring fire. Then she pointed to the center set of doors behind her. Still showering her with his 60-watt smile, Sal commented as he moved past her, "See, that didn't hurt so much, did it?" She followed their progress across the thick carpeting and continued to glare as they knocked twice on the door. Then, not waiting for a response, turned the knob, entered the executive suite, and closed the door.

As Woods and Caruso entered his office, Josh Von Mumser stopped talking to the three people seated at his six person conference table and looked toward them.

"What is this interruption?" he asked. "Who are you? What gives you the right to just barge into my office?" Rather than sounding belligerent, his voice carried true concern.

Moving forward swiftly, Steve handed Josh the warrant with one hand and flipped open his credentials with the other. "Mr. Von Mumser, I am FBI Agent Steve Woods. And this is my partner, Agent Sal Caruso," nodding in Sal's direction. "Mr. Von Mumser, we are here on a personal matter. If it does not bother you to speak in front of your business associates, we can just ask our questions now and be on our way."

The mention of discussing something personal with strangers present got the reaction Woods was expecting. Josh turned back to his associates and terminated the meeting. As he walked his colleagues to the office doors he promised to reschedule the meeting as soon as possible. Remaining at the open door he spoke to his executive secretary, Kate, aka Dragon Lady, to bring in coffee for three. As he said this he looked over his shoulder at Steve and Sal to see if this met with their agreement. Both agents nodded yes.

Coming back into the room, Josh indicated that they sit down at the conference table and he began the conversation. "You said this was about a personal matter yet you came with a warrant. Assuming that I am not under arrest, I am ready to listen."

"No, sir, no arrest that we are aware of," Steve replied. "Mr. Von Mumser, we are here because of some recent unusual events that seem to occur in the area surrounding your father's visits with neighboring states."

At the mention of his father, Josh assumed a more frigid posture and his prior friendly attitude vanished. "Oh? And I would care about my father's activities because? What does his trips, or visits, or schedules have to do with me? In fact, until you mentioned him, I had almost been able to forget I had a father."

"Whoa," Steve thought, "There are some real hostility issues here." Aloud he said, "Well, it seems that, at least recently, whenever he visits a state capitol, dead bodies are found. Seemingly healthy individuals suddenly fall over dead. And the numbers are growing. While we have not been able to isolate the exact cause of the deaths, we are pretty certain they were chemically related. We'll know more after the toxicology tests are completed." At this point Kate entered with the coffee and all talk ceased until she left the office.

"Interesting," Josh commented. "And what does all this have to do with me? Do you think that someone purchased some of my firm's products and used them to commit murder? When you have isolated the chemical involved in the murders, let me know. I can put you in touch with my sales manager and he can go over our records. Other than that, I don't know what else I can help you with." He looked at each man as if his statement might have put an end to the talk.

"Not on your life," Sal thought as he took a sip of his coffee. "Good stuff," he said, "Tastes expensive." Josh just looked at Sal as if the statement did not deserve a comment.

"Mr. Von Mumser, we appreciate your offer of future assistance," Steve said. "But, without intending to pry into family relations, we can't help but sense that you and your father are not very close."

Josh made a snorting sound. "Not close? If I lived on Pluto and he lived on Mercury, we'd still be too close. So, yeah, I guess 'Not close' is a good description. And our familiar circumstances are important for what reason?"

"What we want to know is where you were on these dates." Steve asked as he handed Josh a sheet of paper with the days before, during and after each of his father's out of town trips that started with Delaware.

Josh studied the sheet then looked in astonishment at Steve. "Are you implying that I had something to do with these murders? Because if you are, maybe I need to call my lawyer."

"Sir," Steve said, "You are free to do whatever makes you comfortable. We are not here to arrest you, as we stated earlier, only to ask questions. If your whereabouts on those dates do not present a problem, then telling us now would surely be easier. And better for appearances then for us to escort you out of here to our office. **Then** you would want to call your lawyer. At this time, we are only here fact finding. But, of course, the choice is entirely yours." Steve sat back in his chair and waited for Josh to make a decision, which he seemed to be thinking about.

"Oh, what the hell. I have nothing to hide," Josh began as he looked at both men. "Honestly. I can give you a copy of my appointment book and the telephone numbers of the people I was with. They will confirm our meetings. I can't tell by looking at these dates, but if any of them were weekends, I give you permission to contact my wife. She keeps our social calendar." Josh looked back at the sheet with the dates on it. "The only dates that I can immediately tell you about are the last ones on your list. My wife and I were on a winter vacation for the past ten days. So, we were out of the area."

Sal asked where they went on vacation and were there other people with them. Smiling, Josh told them he took his wife to Hawaii as an anniversary gift. "We stayed at a well known resort on Waikiki Beach. I'm sure someone there saw us. Kate made the reservations, so she can give you the details if needed."

"No, that won't be necessary, thank you." Sal told him and then added, "Happy Anniversary."

"Thank you," Josh replied.

"Mr. Von Mumser, can you tell us what drove this wedge between you and your father?" Sal asked. "He has the reputation of being a pro-rights, people oriented individual. And your employees seem very dedicated to you." Sal noticed the questionable look he got from Josh with that statement. "We were here a few days ago to talk with you. We met a few employees and that was when we learned that you would be back today. I'm surprised the Drag...Kate, didn't tell you about it."

"Actually, she did tell me that a couple of people were here from the federal government. She did not say anything about you being with the FBI. I just assumed it was about one of the many research contracts we have with the government. I am sorry for the confusion." Going on, Josh answered the previous question. "As to what is the issue between me and my father...I have to say that that is very personal. Bottom line, he and I do not agree on what a family is about. I see family as parents, grand-parents, and children. And, if you are lucky, grandchildren.

But behind the labels are people and interactions, love and most important, respect. If you don't respect each other, you don't have a family, you are just a member of a gene pool. My father and I are members of a gene pool. I'm sure there are thousands, maybe millions of families, which have their own form of gene pools. If my father were not the public figure that he is, you would probably not be here or even care about our personal differences.

To cut to the chase, I have lost any respect I ever had for the man and, to me; his indifference towards me demonstrated lack of respect from him. Oh sure, I went through all those childhood phases of trying to measure up to his expectations of me, to make him proud of me. I supported his campaign for statehood. When my grandfather was Mayor of DC we made many family public appearances in a display of unity. I pursued a career in chemical engineering as a means to do scientific research and development for humane services and to gain my father's respect. And, yes, maybe even vocal approval. While I may have accomplished the first two, the last goal never got off the drawing board.

Heck, I even employed his good friend, my god-father, Uncle Bennie. Uncle Bennie has been a blessing. He is an ace chemical scientist and assists me in day-to-day laboratory operations. Uncle Bennie and I are great friends. There have even been times when I wondered how different life would have been if he were my real father." Josh concluded and looking at the two men seemed uncomfortable.

"Sorry about that. Being wistful is generally not something I share. But, for all my efforts, Dear Ole Dad never once said one word of praise. In acknowledgement of my successes, he actually seemed to distance himself more. It was as if the more I achieved, the less he felt he needed to do for or with me. It gave him more time that he could devote to his precious coalition. That was what family meant to him. Having us in the background as a symbol of the great family man while all the while his goals and ambitions came first. Well, I decided that the only way I would ever obtain my goal of peace and respect was to move out. Which is what I did and I have never regretted the choice."

"When did you move out?" Steve asked. "And do you maintain any contact with any family members?"

"It would be about fourteen years ago, shortly after I graduated from college. And yes, I do keep in touch with my mother and sister. In fact, my mother and I have a standing dinner date once a month. The date depends on when her husband is out of town. He travels enough that we know he will be gone at least that often. She calls me, I go pick her up and either take her out or bring her back to my house for dinner with me and my wife."

"We heard that there was a situation with your mother's health that may have contributed to your estrangement from your father," Steve probed.

"Yes," Josh confirmed. "That was the final straw for me. When I left, I begged my mother to come with me. She refused. She said that that man couldn't help being the obsessed person that he was. She blamed my grandfather for starting the pressures that my parents had to live with." He paused for a moment, thinking about the situation and began again.

"Look, let me put it this way. My mother loves my father and will never leave him. When I left home my younger sister was still living at home. She promised to watch out for Mother and to call me if anything happened. My parents seem to survive with whatever arrangement they have. I wish them well, truly. But that is not the life for me."

Looking at each other, Steve spoke for both himself and Sal. "Okay, sir, we really don't have any other questions at this time. If you would have your secretary fax us the pages of your appointment calendar for the dates on that sheet. With the additional information you volunteered, we would appreciate it."

Sal gave Josh his business card with all the numbers on it. "We would like to have your home and cell numbers as well, in case we need to contact you again."

Josh nodded, took a business card from his suit coat pocket and wrote the home and cell information on the back. When he did that, his action triggered a memory in Sal's head that he just could not grab. Sal knew that it would come to him, but that action of Josh's just bothered him. Josh walked them out to the reception area. He gave the sheet of paper to Kate and told her what the agents needed. She was to fax the data as soon as she got it all together. Then Josh stood at the secretary's desk and watched as Steve and Sal got into the elevator to leave.

Neither Steve nor Sal spoke until they had left the building. Having the jobs that they do, they were well aware of potential microphones and cameras being installed in elevators. Once they were out on the street and headed for their car Steve asked Sal, "So, what do you think? Angry enough to try to destroy his father's ambitions?"

Sal kept looking where he was walking, in a hurry to reach their car and get out of the icy wind. "Naw, I heard a little boy back there crying for his father's attention. Shame, that coulda been one happy family if they gave it a try. And, unless he hired someone, that ain't our perp. His days and times were too regulated and recorded. But, I'll let you tell Stella. You have such a way with the ladies." Sal gave Steve a smile that clearly said, "Tag, you're it!"

Chapter XX

January 27, 2015
Atlanta, Georgia and Washington, DC

Maris Ayin's Office, Atlanta, Georgia

Maris went over the test results one more time. Twenty-two people, all with the same symptoms of death and no one culprit identified. She was extremely frustrated. She had placed all the systems into a National Priorities List site generated by the Environmental Protection Agency. Of some fifteen hundred and eighty-five EPA sites no clear matches were identified. This was not getting them any closer to a possible cause or antidote. "Misery loves company," she thought as she reached for the telephone to share the most recent results with Stella.

She was in luck when Stella answered on the second ring. She heard the hopeful sound in Stella's voice that would not be there after she gave her report. "Stella, I only have an update for you, nothing final. I am giving you the bottom line up front so you won't have any false expectations from this call. Are you okay with that?"

There was an audible sigh at the other end of the line. "Maris, any news at this point is more news than I currently have. We have been running into so many dead ends; excuse the phrase that I'm ready to believe in voodoo doll spells or aliens with dead earthling fetishes. So, let me have it. Tell me what you have learned."

"Okay. I could not find any known chemical in any digestive track, no puncture marks as point of entry, and the one diabetic was the lone exception with insulin injection marks. There were no suspicious or unusual marks, rashes, or bruising to indicate any absorption through the skin." Maris paused and Stella could hear the rustling of papers. "From the lack of arterial deterioration, something that takes time to happen, I believe the internal shutdown occurred over a short period of time. Perhaps from a few minutes to a few hours, no more." Not wanting to stop for any interruptions or questions, Maris rapidly continued the conversation.

"We have performed all the current tests known for deaths of this questionable nature and have come up blank. We even enlisted the aid of ATSDR for analyses."

Here Stella did cut in. "ATSDR? What is that, a computer program?"

"No," Maris told her, "It stands for Agency for Toxic Substances and Disease Registry. ATSDR is mandated by Congress to perform specific functions concerning the effect on public health of hazardous substances in the environment. The regional level here is staffed within the Atlanta EPA Regional office. For me it was like getting the help of two agencies for the price of one. Anyway, unless there is some precise element that we are looking for, I can only continue to repeat the test with degrees of variance until, hopefully, something stands out amongst all our victims." As she made that comment, a new thought occurred to Maris. "You know, maybe I have been going at this all wrong. Maybe I need to look for variance instead of commonality. I'll keep you informed of all test results."

"Thank Maris. I know you are doing all you can. I just can't help feeling like I'm racing against the clock to catch this guy before he strikes again. We have the method—poison; we have the means—public gatherings, but what we don't have is the motive. That is still up for grabs. We thought we were on to something with Von Mumser's son. They are not on the best of terms. Heck, they aren't on any terms at all. From our investigation it seems they haven't met or spoken in over a decade. But, the son owns a pharmaceutical firm and we had to check him out. He has iron clad alibis for every date. So, now we are back to square one and eager to move forward. Anything you find will be appreciated. I'll let you know if we come up with anything at this end. Happy hunting," Stella said as she ended the call.

Stella Vega's Office, FBI Building, Washington, DC

After her conversation with Maris, Stella began thinking ahead. The only common thread they had was the Coalition Chairman, Richard Von Mumser. Whoever was committing these murders was using Von Mumser's state visits as a cover. She acknowledged that this person was very good, having gone undetected so far. Maybe he was a disguise artist and we need to review the tapes for height, build, walk, or facial similarities.

Stella decided her side needed to be one step ahead of this person. If Richard Von Mumser was the catalyst, she needed to know what his travel schedule was. She needed to know which state he planned to visit next. Then she was going to ensure that the building was covered from top to bottom with every form of local and federal law and drug enforcement. She rifled through her purse until she found the business card she was looking for. Picking up the telephone, she dialed the cell phone number hand written on the card.

Jack Yu answered on the third ring. "Jack, this is Stella Vega, from the FBI. We met in Connecticut a few weeks ago."

Jack wasted no time to confirm the meeting. "Yes, Ms. Vega, I clearly remember the meeting. Have you called with some good news? Have you caught the person who is doing this?"

"No," Stella told him, "And that is why I am calling. Can you tell me the next state that Mr. Von Mumser is scheduled to visit? And the date of the visit would be helpful."

"Sure, that is easy. He is planning to go to Massachusetts on February 9th. That is if the trip is not cancelled. It seems that Governor Matsangakis is a little nervous about having the Chairman come there. Given the circumstances that have occurred during the recent state trips, I can understand the governor's trepidation.

Personally, I would prefer to see all upcoming trips cancelled until this nutcase is captured. The chairman believes that if he altered his schedule in any way, then this criminal has achieved the upper hand. What do you think?"

"Jack," Stella said, "I am sorry to disappoint you, but I agree with your boss. In fact, I would like to have a talk with him. Today, if possible."

Jack was delighted to be of some help, in any form. He was also eager to see Stella again. She was the type of no-nonsense, confident female that he admired. She was his ideal female of brains and beauty. "The Chairman will be at his office in the Coalition building this afternoon, at about two o'clock. I can see that you have time with him then. Is that a good time for you?"

"Perfect, I'll be there at two. And, Jack, thank you."

"Your welcome, Stella, anytime," Jack replied as he snapped his cell phone closed. He knew there was a smile on his face, but he glanced in the rear view mirror to confirm just how wide the smile was. It was wide.

Two P.M., Coalition Headquarters, 16th Street, NW, Washington, DC

Jack met Stella at the door and escorted her into Von Mumser's office. He was going to introduce Stella to his boss when she took over that formality. Von Mumser was seated at his desk and rose to meet Stella when she entered the room. Moving forward to meet him halfway, Stella introduced herself and showed him her badge. "Thank you for seeing me on such short notice, Mr. Von Mumser. I know what a busy schedule you must have."

"Not at all, Agent Vega, the pleasure is mine. Anything I can do to assist the authorities will be a privilege. Please, have a seat." He indicated a chair in a seating area against the far wall. There were four chairs surrounding an elaborate glass inlaid cherry wood coffee table. Stella took the seat against the wall. Von Mumser sat in the chair to her right which had him facing the office entrance in the event anyone came in. Jack sat across from Stella with his appointment book in hand, ready to take notes or provide any required information.

Von Mumser opened the conversation. "Jack tells me you want to talk about my upcoming trip to Massachusetts. What is it I can help you with?"

"Yes sir, thank you. I do want to discuss your next trip. I understand that the governor of Massachusetts might be thinking of canceling, or postponing the visit. While I might be able to understand his concern, I don't think that either option would solve the problem. We need to get this person. If it isn't in Massachusetts, due to cancellation, it will continue at some other capitol location. We would rather stop this person sooner rather than later. We would like to help you to ensure that the Massachusetts trip is not delayed."

"Interesting," was Von Mumser's immediate response. "How do you propose to ensure that the Massachusetts trip goes according to schedule?"

"Well, with your permission, we are ready to contact the governor's office to convince them to keep the visit on track. You see Mr. Von Mumser; we believe that someone is using your trips as a cover to commit murder. Whether for some form of personal gain or to cause some shadow of doubt on either you or your campaign goal, is something I cannot pinpoint. The exact reason for this mayhem eludes us but we feel your trip to Massachusetts is a good way to detect, or expose, and hopefully, arrest the person responsible for these deaths. I know that you have legitimate business to discuss with the governor, which we do not wish to alter. In fact, we really prefer you to maintain your regular routine."

Von Mumser looked at Stella as if seeing her for the very first time. "Excuse me? Do you really think that someone is shadowing my business trips to kill people? Isn't that just a bit bizarre? After all, I have been to many states and important political function where nothing happened to anyone. Are you so certain about this murderer?"

"Well, Sir, we can never be absolutely sure of anything. But we do have a hunch about this case and need your cooperation to see it through."

"Of course, Agent Vega, whatever you think is best. I just don't understand what you are going to do to catch this person. What do you want me or Governor Matsangakis to do?"

"We only want you and the governor to perform normal business functions. We would have the place covered with agents and everyone entering and exiting the building will be photographed. Plus, everyone will have to go through a metal detector. No bags, backpacks, or purses will be allowed in. We will try not to interfere with the daily official business at the capitol. We will be watching all the people who gather around you when you do your public appearance. We would be within calling distance at all times. We do not intend to place you in any dangerous situation."

Von Mumser looked from Stella, who waited for his reply, to Jack, who was slowly nodding at his boss to accept the offer. Returning his attention to Stella, he gave his okay for her to contact Governor Matsangakis. He told Stella that Jack had all the details for the visit and the people she will need to contact. He told her if there was anything else she found that she needed from him to just call. As Von Mumser stood up, she knew the meeting was over. She stood as well, thanked Von Mumser, shook his hand in farewell, and made to leave the room. Jack told Stella he would see her out and they could stop by his office for the Massachusetts details. She then followed Jack out of one office and into another.

Jack seemed a little nervous when he gathered the information for Stella. He actually dropped the papers twice when handing them to Stella. Finally, as he was walking her to the building entrance, he stopped and waited for Stella to notice. She turned back to Jack and asked if there was a problem.

"No, no problem," Jack said. "I was just wondering if you might have time to go for a coffee. There's a coffee shop a few blocks away."

Smiling, Stella thanked him but said she had tons more work to do when she got back to her office. She did give Jack a tiny hint of encouragement by telling him that they should probably put the offer off until the case was over. Jack seemed to be satisfied with that and watched as she left the building and descended the steps.

Stella Vega's Office, FBI Building, Washington, DC

Back at her desk, Stella called Sal and Steve. She told them about her plan to try to flush out the killer during Von Mumser's upcoming trip to Massachusetts. She told them she was going to fax the trip details to them and needed them to contact the Massachusetts protocol personnel. She wanted the state to understand what the Bureau was going to do and for the visit not to be cancelled. She told them that it was important enough that if they had to go face-to-face with the folks in Massachusetts, the travel expenses would be covered. That seemed to please Steve's accountant side. Steve told her that he and Sal would drive to Boston first thing in the morning.

Chapter XXI

February 6, 2015
State Capitol Building
Boston, Massachusetts

The day started very early for Steve and Sal. They had assured Governor Matsangakis that they would be in attendance when Von Mumser arrived. The meeting was scheduled for ten a.m. They decided the distance was close enough to drive. Even calculating for a rest stop, they would be at the capitol building by nine. Steve felt good about the road conditions, all clear, plus there was no road construction to delay the drive. They actually arrived at the Boston city limits at eight-forty in the morning. That was when the good driving conditions changed.

With the traffic congestion and the in-city road work, Steve still figured they would make their appointment with time to spare. They knew from an earlier cell phone call that Stella was already on site. She told them that all extra security was in place and all was going well. Now all they had to do was get to the capitol building. To Sal it seemed there was a traffic light at every corner. They were second in line at a traffic signal when the traffic light ahead turned green. The car in front of them was not moving so Steve honked to get the driver going. The action worked and they moved on.

"Sal, did you notice the license plates on that car?" Not waiting for a reply, Steve went on. "The plates are from Delaware. The motto on the plate is: Delaware, The First State."

"Yeah, so?" Sal asked.

"Oh, nothing," Steve answered. "I was just wondering. If Delaware is the first state, which is the second state?"

"I dunno. Whadda ya need to know for?" Sal asked.

"Just help me out here, okay? Which state is the second one?" Steve persisted.

"Say, man, what is this? Some kind of citizenship test? Do you know long it's been since I was in school? No, don't answer that. Okay, okay, gimme a minute to think." Sal paused for a short while to think about the question.

"Well, I can't swear, but I believe that Pennsylvania is the second state."

"How sure?" Steve asked, "Because that is what I was thinking too, Pennsylvania."

"Well, now that I am remembering my elementary school lessons, or recalling something I saw on the History Channel about Ben Franklin; Old Benjamin Franklin was really pissed off because Delaware signed first. So, yeah, I'm pretty sure Pennsylvania was second."

"Great, Sal, we may have a break here. If Delaware is first, and Pennsylvania is second, I'll lay odds that New Jersey is third. That being so, then Massachusetts is sixth and we need to know which one is seventh. That would be the next state. Now, what we would need to know is the date. That might give us an advantage. I hate this useless felling of coming to a play during the second act. We need to be there from the beginning and see everything and everyone for ourselves."

"Well," Sal began, "If we're going to get any kind of a break, today would be a good day for that to happen."

"Yeah, I agree," Steve said as he watched the state capitol building come into view. "Well, here we are. Stella said there would be a parking space for us. Sure glad about that, this place looks real packed today." Then, as an after thought, Steve told Sal, "Oh, yeah, remind me to tell Stella about what state may be next if the deaths don't stop here today." Sal nodded agreement.

Steve showed his badge to the security guard at the gated parking area. After they parked the car and were walking toward the building, Steve looked at Sal and said, "Okay, partner, its show time."

The state capitol building for Massachusetts used the Federal style of construction. The fifty-nine foot structure sported a gold gilded dome and cupola. It never ceased to amuse and frustrate Richard Von

Mumser how many capitol buildings seemed to be congruent with the capitol building in Washington, DC. Ironic would be a more apropos word. All these states emulated the one place in the United States of America where the citizens could not claim statehood. Hopefully, he told himself, he would be the man to change that situation.

It was very obvious to anyone in or around the building today that security was quite high. Not only were there extra police from Boston, both in and outside, it appeared that all capitol security was on duty. The governor had called last week to suggest that their meeting be rearranged to an unannounced alternate date. Von Mumser, with the aid of the FBI, had successfully convinced Governor Matsangakis it would serve no purpose. If there truly was someone trailing his activities, it was clearly someone either having inside information or, the ability to get into computer networks and acquire the information. Besides, it would be an ideal situation, with the heightened security and the FBI presence to either capture this person or convince him "the jig is up" and these deaths would cease.

Governor Petros "Pierre" Matsangakis was more at ease knowing that there were probably going to be more security personnel at the capitol today than visitors. It was most important that no one be harmed. Governor Matsangakis, a first generation American and, a life long Bostonian, was totally dedicated to the Commonwealth of Massachusetts and all its citizens.

America was the country of choice for his father, fleeing from Nazi controlled Greece during World War II. His father loved this country and more importantly, he loved Boston. This was where he met his beautiful wife, Elena. His father never let anyone, including himself and his three brothers, forget how great this country is and how people had the opportunity to do and be anything they desired in America. The governor learned that lesson well and worked very hard to keep those opportunities and privileges available to the citizens. He would not deliberately put anyone's safety at risk.

By the appointed time for the meeting, the FBI had several agents on location. Rightfully so, since both the governor and the Coalition Chairman had received assurances of complete coverage. No one was going to get either into the building or near Von Mumser without having undergone a rigorous security screening. Today, no backpacks, briefcases or large purses were allowed in the visitors' area. The increased number of reporters that were now following Von Mumser's state visits was limited to a small number. Governor Matsangakis did not want this visit to turn into a three ring circus.

Matsangakis was concerned that all the activity surrounding his visitor was going to detract from the celebrations already planned to observe the Commonwealth's anniversary. He liked Richard Von Mumser and had great respect for the man and his cause. Yet, today, he just wanted the visit over and done with. He knew that Von Mumser and his group were in the building and on the way to his office. Agents Vega, Woods, and Caruso were already in his waiting area. They were going to remain there, with Richard's party, while he and Von Mumser had their talk. Then the agents were going to escort Richard and his group to the visitors' area. Pierre had gone to church this morning to say a special prayer for peace. He was about to see how powerful that prayer was.

Richard Von Mumser, Jack Yu, and Julius Walsh were directed to the governor's suite. The political science interns, who assisted Von Mumser on this trip, were left in the visitors' area to assemble their materials on two assigned tables for that purpose. Four local police officers, assigned to watch over the campaign tables, both assisted and looked through the paperwork that would be handed out later in the day.

As Richard entered Governor Petros "Pierre" Matsangakis' anteroom area, he was greeted by the six foot three inch, two hundred and sixty pound governor himself. In a traditional Greek greeting, the governor came across the room, embraced Von Mumser and kissed the air next to each cheek. Von Mumser returned the gesture. Backing up from the personal closeness, Matsangakis shook Von Mumser' hand. "Yassou, my friend. Welcome! Massachusetts is honored by your presence today."

"Efkaristo," Von Mumser replied.

"Come my friend, lets go into my office where we can have some privacy", Matsangakis stated as he walked with Von Mumser towards his office.

Before they reached the double doors into the governor's private office, he turned and spoke to his personal assistant, Andreas Komninos, "Andreas, sass-parakalo, bring some coffee and baklava for our guests." He indicated those remaining in the anteroom. "And some for me and Richard also." Turning more to face those remaining in the room, he added, "Before you feel any inclination to refuse, you should know that my own mother made the baklava and she would take it as an insult if anyone didn't at least try the Greek specialty."

Stella spoke for the group. "We wouldn't think of insulting your mother. I, personally, am looking forward to tasting the home made treat. Thank you…. Err, Efkaristo, for your hospitality."

"Parakalo. You're welcome." Matsangakis responded. Then he and Von Mumser left the waiting area, entered his office and he closed the doors.

Left to wait for the meeting to be over, Stella decided to go over all the precautions that had been put in place. The amount of security impressed Jack. Julius was actively taking photos and notes that he planned to use pending Agent Vega's okay. Jack voiced his concerns that maybe this was someone who was jealous of the good work that the Chairman is doing, and has done, for all the residents of the District. He stated that the Chairman was a super guy and pointed out that all the Von Mumser family money and standing did not turn the Chairman's head away from the people. Jack reminded everyone that Von Mumser donated his own time and money in his efforts to seek statehood. "The Chairman comes from good roots, his father was a former Mayor of DC, and he, himself, is a member of numerous civic organizations," Jack commented.

Seeing that he had everyone's attention, he pushed on to ensure they had a full picture of the man he worked for. "He served his country as a member of the DC Army National Guard and even saw action when stationed in Kuwait. It is so frustrating to see the dedication the Chairman displayed and to think that someone was out there trying to undermine his efforts with these senseless killings." The others let Jack ramble on, making sympathetic comments or noises.

Jack's grand standing was interrupted by the arrival of the coffee and pastry. Jack made it a point to sit next to Stella. When she looked at him, Jack smiled and said, "Do you think we can consider this our cup of coffee together?"

"Nice try Jack. But, as I told you before, if we have coffee, that will have to wait until this case is solved." Jack drew some hope from that remark and remained silent. For the remainder of their wait they exchanged small talk about what they should be looking for when they went out for the public appearance.

Twenty-five minutes after Von Mumser and Matsangakis went into the governor's office, the doors opened and both men came out smiling. The governor apologized for taking up so much of their time. He asked if the baklava met everyone's expectation and was very pleased with all the compliments. He promised to relay their pleasure to his mother. He then walked the group to the office suite's main entrance and shook hands with each person as they entered the hallway.

The group moved downstairs to the section of the visitors' area reserved for the set up of Von Mumser's literature. The line of people waiting to shake hands and speak with Von Mumser seemed longer than normal. A lot of people appeared intent on telling him that he was doing a good thing and that they supported his cause. The law enforcement agents stayed close to Von Mumser and closely watched each person as they approached him.

Steve stood with Jack who was avidly looking at each person's face to see if he recognized anyone. Sal moved around the room with Julius as he photographed the crowd and each person Von Mumser spoke with. Julius was determined to photo as much of the crowd as possible. Stella stayed in the background surveying the people for anything unusual. The interns carried out their responsibilities of handing out statehood campaign literature and signing people up for future communications.

Von Mumser, for his part, appeared relaxed and very comfortable with all the attention. He seemed interested in making contact with native Bay Staters and especially with life long Bostonians. These he spent a little more time with, expounding on the importance of having statehood. As was his habit, he asked numerous people if they had a favorite local restaurant they would recommend. Others he asked if they had heard of any of the places on a list of eateries that he had brought with him, asking for directions.

When the allotted hour was over, all seemed fine. No suspicious activities and no bodies lying around. The FBI agents escorted Von Mumser and his group out of the building and into their waiting transportation. Von Mumser and company had been gone for some forty-five minutes when the first man collapsed on the floor of the visitors' area. The building was immediately sealed. No one out and no one in, except for medical and emergency personnel.

Within three hours of Von Mumser's departure, there were six bodies literally lining the halls of the state capitol. All Caucasian and all male. EMS personnel examined each breathing person before clearing him or her to leave. The bodies were moved to a storage area in the back of the building, but were not to be removed until a CDC agent arrived to oversee the autopsies.

Stella commandeered all the security tapes and called ahead to Washington to have an agent meet Von Mumser's train at Union Station. She wanted Jack Yu put on notice to come into her office tomorrow morning for an interview. Plus, she told her Washington office, if Mr. Yu appeared to give any resistance to this direction, they were at liberty to place Mr. Yu under house arrest and have someone stay the night with him and escort him to her office in the morning.

She was inconsolable. Steve and Sal had never seen her so upset or angry. When they tried to talk with her, she was short and sharp. "How did this happen?" And then, "This was not supposed to happen." Another pause, and then in rapid fire stated, "What did I do wrong?" "Who is this person?" "What drug is he using?" "How is he doing this?" "I want this guy!!"

She realized that she had to regroup and get back on track. She ordered all the security personnel, with the tapes, to gather in the conference room after the building had been emptied of all civilians. She had Sal and Steve remain on the ground floor with the Boston agents to oversee the bodies and CSI activities. But, she knew her immediate responsibility was to see Governor Matsangakis. Not something she was looking forward to.

As she approached his office, she took several deep breaths to steady her nerves. Stepping into the waiting area, she was met by the governor's assistant, Andreas. He told her the governor was expecting her. She was to go on into his office. She nodded her understanding to Andreas and went to enter Matsangakis' office.

As she entered the governor's private office, Matsangakis was on the phone. When he looked up and saw her, he waved her into the chair next to his desk and continued speaking into the phone. "Yes, a full list of the victims and their next-of-kin, as soon as possible." He paused to listen to the speaker. "No, no delays. I will be here until you have the information. Call me immediately." He paused again for the person on the other end. "Yes, my private line. Thank you." He ended the call and just looked at his hand as it remained on the telephone. Stella knew he was collecting his thoughts before speaking to her.

A few minutes passed before he shifted his view to her. Remaining seated, he placed his hands on his knees and swiveled his chair to fully face her. "Agent Vega, tell me you have identified this maniac and are going to make an arrest."

She looked into his eyes that seemed to have aged ten years since this morning, "I'm sorry, Governor, I can not say that right now. I want you to know how terribly sorry I am about this. There is nothing I can say or do to explain how this happened."

"How comforting. I'm sure the family members will find that reassuring." Matsangakis responded. "I had placed my faith, and my citizens' lives, in your hands. If you recall, I wanted to postpone this visit. It was based your assurances that allowed me to let the meeting occur. And now six Massachusetts residents have paid for my mistake. How am I supposed to live with that?"

Stella heard the misery in Matsangakis' voice, even though outwardly he remained calm. "I know this is not going to ease the families' sorrow; but I honestly believe that this tragedy would have happened with or without the visit today."

Matsangakis looked stunned, "What do you mean?"

"I mean," Stella explained, "that we think this person has been using Von Mumser's schedule to commit these murders. So, whether Von Mumser came or not, this person would have come here today because that was his original date. Von Mumser was the cover, not the reason. It was neither your fault nor Von Mumser's that this person is out to commit murder. Actually, because Von Mumser did come today, we now have extensive coverage, including security tapes. I promise you that we are going to study every inch of those tapes and if anything, and I do mean anything, shows up, we will take immediate action. Governor, you did nothing wrong and you need to understand that."

Matsangakis sat silently for a few minutes just looking at Stella. Then he slowly nodded his understanding, took Stella's hands in his and commented, "Efkaristo Agent Vega, you have eased my pain. Please, keep me informed of your progress." Rising, he escorted Stella out of his office and into the anteroom area where his executive assistant waited. Matsangakis told Andreas to see Stella to the conference room where the others had gathered and to give any assistance needed. The governor remained behind as he watched the other two leave the room.

Chapter XXII

February 6, 2015
Conference Room
State Capitol Building
Boston, Massachusetts

When Stella entered the conference room all the buzzing stopped as all eyes turned to her. Every seat at the table was occupied plus many more chairs were lining the sidewalls. She walked to the far end of the long over conference table. When she stood at the lectern placed there, her back was to the video screen occupying that wall. She maintained silence as she scanned the faces in front of her. As if making a decision, she spoke.

"Agent Woods is everyone here that participated in today's security?"

"Yes ma'am. All forty six of us, including yourself."

Stella nodded at the reply. Then the next question came. "Agent Caruso, do you have all the security tapes from today?"

"Yes ma'am," came the reply. "From all eight cameras."

"Good. Now let me tell you what we are going to do. Without the pop-corn, we are going to watch each security tape. For the first sweep, we are going to study those cameras that covered the visitors' gallery from the time of Mr. Von Mumser's appearance until his departure. The first viewing will be at regular speed. Everyone is to watch and take notes. If you have a question, speak up and the technician will stop the video. I don't care how long it takes. We can take ten minute breaks after each viewing. I have made arrangements to have light snacks and drinks sent in. I am most interested in anything that looks odd, or out of place, to any of you. Anything at all. Don't wait, speak up. Everyone got that?" She received total agreement.

"Okay, you all have notepads and pens. So, let's begin." As Stella noted to the technician to start the first tape she spotted the D.C. Daily reporter, Julius Walsh, seated in a chair closest to the door. "One moment please, don't start the tape yet," she instructed the technician as she moved away from the lectern and advanced to where Julius sat and stopped in front of him. In a lowered voice she spoke to him. "Mr. Walsh, would you come out into the hallway with me?"

While it may have sounded like a question to anyone listening, Julius knew a command when he heard it. "Certainly, Agent Vega," he replied as he rose and followed her out of the room.

In the hallway Stella wasted no time. "Mr. Walsh, may I ask how you happen to be in a room full of security personnel? This is a highly sensitive Closed Door meeting."

"Yes ma'am, I know. I spoke with Agent Woods about our agreement for my exclusive coverage of this case. Agent Vega, I know that anything you learn in that room will not be printable for me. At least not at this time. That was our understanding. And, in order to have a completely covered story, I do need to be where the news is happening. Also part of our agreement. Plus, one added feature for you is my reporter's instinct to see and question people and situations. I may be an asset to you in there. While all of you, good as you are, will be looking through a legal lens, I would not. I would be looking for the story. Agent Woods agreed with me when we spoke. Don't worry; he reiterated the verbal contract we have about nothing going to press without your approval."

Stella could see the logic in Julius' argument and mentally concurred that his view of the tapes might be an advantage. He would watch them from a different angle than the trained law enforcement perspective. "Okay, Mr. Walsh, you may stay in the room. As long as you maintain your end of our agreement, nothing printed without approval, we will get along fine." Julius nodded his head in understanding as the two re-entered the conference room.

Stella thanked everyone for their patience and told the video technician to start the first designated tape. In total, there were eight security cameras operating today. There were four cameras covering the visitors' gallery on this day when there are normally only three. The added camera provided a three hundred and sixty-degree view. The viewing of the four cameras took over three hours. Each tape was stopped, rewound and slowly forwarded each time one of the victims appeared.

The group was given short ten minute breaks between tapes and then continued to view and review the gallery videos. Without conscience awareness, a thought occurred to Julius during the second viewing of the tapes.

"Uh, Agent Vega? I have a question, please," Julius stated as he stood up. For some reason Julius felt like a small child trying to please the teacher.

"Yes, Mr. Walsh? Your question please," Stella answered.

Nervous as the school boy that he felt like, he stumbled over his question. "Yes, well, I just had a thought, that may not really be anything of importance, that is. But, I was just…thinking, as we watched the tapes…" at this point he just stopped talking and looked at Stella as if he needed encouragement.

"My G-d," Stella thought, "finally, someone notices something and he's going to ramble on forever." Aloud she asked, "Yes, Mr. Walsh, you have a question?"

Julius knew that he looked silly to all those law enforcement officers in the room. "Some Ace reporter I make," ran through his head. Outwardly he nodded his head once and just plunged forward. "Yes, well, what I saw, what we all saw, was Mr. Von Mumser meeting and greeting a lot of people. Those people whom he handed his business card to, and were not identified as victims, got a card from his right suit pocket or, from one of his assistants. Yet, it seemed that when he handed a card to any of those who died, it was from his left suit pocket.

I know that that action may not mean anything. You know, some cards from one pocket and some from the other. And, Mr. Von Mumser was pretty busy with so many people. But, I also noticed that the people with cards from the right pocket got to keep the cards. And those who handled the cards from the left pocket gave the cards back or, Mr. Von Mumser took the card back. I really couldn't tell. Do you know if any of the victims had a card on them when you found them?" When Julius had finished speaking he continued to stand and looked at Stella. She was looking at him as if in shock, so he sat down.

That's it, Sal thought. The same motion Josh Von Mumser made when he gave us his business card from his suit pocket. Just like his old man. No wonder the action seemed so familiar.

Stella mentally felt as if her mouth were hanging open. She was amazed. Walsh had made a great observation. How had they, all trained professionals, missed something so obvious? Giving herself a mental shake, she responded to Julius' statement.

"Mr. Walsh that was an excellent observation. Thank you." She then directed the video technician to rerun one tape until one of the victims appeared with Mr. Von Mumser, then to rewind the tape to the previous person. The process was to go forward, slowly, from the prior person, to the victim and then on to the next person with Mr. Von Mumser. She told the technician that she wanted this view for each of the victims as they were captured on tape.

The entire group watched the reviewing of one tape several times. Then another of the tapes, from another angle was watched again, with the same results. None of the victims left Von Mumser's presence with a card. Stella had one officer check the lists of property found on each victim and soon learned that none listed any card from Von Mumser.

Nothing else of suspicion was noted on any of the remaining security tapes that were viewed. Stella asked each person to make an after-action report detailing what duty they had today, what they observed, and their impressions from viewing the tapes. She asked to have their reports so soon as possible, but not later than three days out. She advised them not to discuss this case with anyone else and that if any other thoughts came to anyone, to contact her or her team immediately.

"And people," she advised, "As I told Governor Matsangakis, do not for one minute think that what happened today had anything to with how you did or did not perform. Regardless of how much we planned, we were dealing with a very clever, accomplished killer. But, no matter how clever, he will make a mistake and we will be there to take advantage of it. I sincerely appreciate all your efforts and eagerly look forward to reading your reports. Meeting over. Thank you," she concluded. She instructed the video technician to give the tapes to Agent Caruso. Then she told Woods, Caruso, Walsh, and the Capitol Police Chief to remain behind.

She remained behind the lectern until all the others had left the room. She then spoke to the police officer. "Chief, do you have a secured room where we can talk?" He told her that he did and then led the group to his office in the building. After everyone was seated in his small twelve-by-twenty foot office, at a small round four person table, Stella took over the gathering.

"Okay, something is getting to these people. And someone has been able to avoid dozens of trained personnel. Steve, Sal," she spoke directly to them, "I need you two in Washington tomorrow morning, bright and early. We have an appointment with Mr. Yu and I'd appreciate it if you two would take responsibility for the security tapes and transport them for me." There was no inquiry in her tone, it was clearly a directive.

She then focused her attention on the police chief. "Chief, I understand that a regional CDC representative and an ATSDR investigator are here to take over the autopsy responsibilities?"

"Yes ma'am. They are having the bodies moved to one of their facilities. As an added clean air measure, they are going to chemically clean the building's air system over night. They assured me that all their present readings were in the clean air zone, but they were going to do the filtering as an added measure and to appease public concern."

"That sounds fine." Stella commented, and then added, "Please see that Ms. Maris Ayin from the Atlanta Regional CDC is informed of the autopsy results. She is the lead disease and toxicology individual on this case. She may require your assistance. I will give you her office telephone information." She wrote the number on a paper and then handed it to him.

Now her attention turned to Julius. "Mr. Walsh, I need you to return to your office in DC, develop your film and meet us in my office at approximately nine tomorrow morning. Plus, as you know, other than the obvious information that everyone saw out in the gallery, you cannot print anything you saw or heard in the conference room." Not waiting for his response, she continued. "I do need you to write down an after action report of what you saw, or heard, today. Do include your observation about the cards in Von Mumser's left jacket pocket. As we promised, when this case is concluded, you are to have exclusive reporting rights. Should those cards become something of significance, your report will serve as documentation that the original thought was yours."

Julius was very pleased that she had reinforced his role in this case and told Stella he would see her in the morning and, unless she needed him for anything else, he was going to catch the next train back to DC. She told him he could leave and asked the police chief if he had someone to drive Julius to the station. She did not want Julius to be surrounded by other reporters trying to break him down. A ride was arranged and Julius left.

Sal, still seated to Stella's left, suddenly snapped his fingers as if he just remembered something. That drew Stella's attention. "You got something Sal?"

"I'm not sure Stella, but any idea is better than empty air, right?"

"Out with it Sal, I'm way too tired to play twenty questions."

Sal proceeded to tell her about Steve's idea about the order of the states being targets. "If Delaware was first and Pennsylvania was second, and now if Massachusetts was sixth, we might know which state would be next," Sal repeated from his earlier conversation with Steve. Stella liked the idea and told Sal to check it out and let her know.

It was now quite late in the evening. There did not seem to be any more business for this night. Stella told the Chief to let her know of any new developments. She then told her team to go home and she would see them in the morning. The guys wanted to see her to her hotel, but she declined. She told them she was going to hang around the building awhile to see how things were going with the Crime Scene Investigators and the coroners. The guys left her with the police chief and went to their car to start their return trip.

Stella asked the Chief to show her where the bodies had been placed, and then followed him out of his office. "Thank G-d I love caffeine so much. I'm going to be drinking tons of the stuff to just get through this night," she thought as they walked down the now empty hallway.

Chapter XXIII

February 7, 2015
Caption in USA Today's
State-by-State Column

MASSACHUSETTS:
Capitol killer strikes again. Yesterday six bodies were discovered in the state capitol building in Boston. They mirrored those deaths in Delaware, Pennsylvania, New Jersey, Georgia, and Connecticut; no outward signs for the cause of death. Theories are mounting that this is the work of one person. Authorities have declined to comment at this point. The FBI and CDC are working closely with local law enforcement agencies from each municipality involved.

Chapter XXIV

February 7, 2015
Stella Vega's Office
FBI Building
Washington, DC

Stella got into her office at eight fifteen in the morning. Julius was already there. She was told that Jack would in at nine and that Steve and Sal were on their way, by plane, and would be there by ten.

Julius sat across from Stella at a small round table in her office. He gave her all the prints from the cameras he used yesterday. While Stella looked over the prints, Julius lamented about a talk he had with his editor, Don Wellen. "Yeah, he was pretty angry with me last night. He said all I could do was take pretty pictures of Von Mumser with no in-depth details of what was going on. I had to do some fancy talking to convince him that I was right where the action was—with Von Mumser. After all, the bodies only seem to fall when he is in town."

Julius, like Jack, believed that someone else was doing this to Von Mumser, possibly to cast the Chairman in doubt. "I told Mr. Wellen I needed to be **the** reporter on the scene when the killer was captured. I reminded him of our agreement with you that this would be a scoop that the Daily could ill afford to lose out on." He told her that Wellen wanted to know what state Von Mumser was going to visit next.

"Based on my talk with Jack this morning, Von Mumser is very disturbed with these incidents and all the negative attention he is getting. Von Mumser plans to take a break and stay in DC for a while. He is hoping that this will deter the killer in some way and, hopefully, these deaths will stop." Julius stopped to replenish his lungs than drove on. "My new orders from Mr. Wellen are to stick like glue to Von Mumser. I just know there is a Nobel Prize story here."

Stella sensed Julius' excitement in now being able to fully concentrate on his documentary of Von Mumser's campaign and all the side issues. She was happy for this eager guy, but wanted to make sure that he didn't give away any clues that might make the killer suspicious. "Mr. Walsh, I am pleased that we will be working together. I just hope that we will both have our successes sooner rather than later. I need to reiterate our pact that nothing is printed about close-hold information without our okay."

"Oh yes ma'am. Trust me that is upper most in my mind with every word I write." Julius told her that the prints he brought today were copies and her's to keep. He was eager to get back to this office to go through all his older shots, to see if he had anything else he could share. When he told this to Stella, she told him it was a good plan. She thanked him again for his help. She rose from her chair, shook his hand and walked him out of her office. She had a security guard escort Julius out of the building. She stood in the hallway of her office until the elevator doors closed.

Jack arrived at five minutes after nine without his attorney. When Stella asked if the lawyer, Mr. Pugh, was going to be coming, Jack told her that it was just him. He told her he had nothing to hide and wanted to prove it. When she asked how his boss was doing this morning, Jack told her that Von Mumser was locked in his coalition office and not seeing anyone.

"The chairman just cannot believe that this curse is continuing," Jack told her. To Jack these killings just proved that someone is out to discredit the Chairman. When Jack asked if there had been any arrests, he was visibly disappointed that there had been no capture. "What is the problem? Obviously the killer was there yesterday. Why was there no arrest?" Jack bemoaned to any one listening. "I'm sorry, my emotions just got the better of me," he told Stella. "What can I do for you today?"

Stella told him that she wanted him to view the security tapes from yesterday but they were in the possession of Steve and Sal, who would not be arriving for about another hour. She asked him if he would be able to wait. Jack said he could wait and would she like to have a coffee. Stella smiled and told Jack she would like a coffee and bagel. She told him there was a small sandwich shop on the first floor.

When Jack returned with the food, they sat at Stella's small table to eat and await Steve and Sal. That was where they were seated when Maris called.

Stella put her on the speaker and told Maris that Jack Yu was in the room. Maris told them that there was nothing new to report and now she had to add six more analyses to put through the same testing. Maris said that she needed a clue, anything to lead her in a new direction. She was frustrated with all the negative results. She told them that once she was able to isolate the chemical she would know the associated risks to the individual and the public at large.

Jack, listening to the conversation, asked to say something. Stella told him it was okay. Jack told them that if they were stumped for chemical clues that they could possibly ask his boss for advice.

"Why would I ask Mr. Von Mumser for advice?" Maris questioned.

"Because of his background and training." Jack replied.

"Explain, please." Maris asked.

"Gladly," Jack answered. "Mr. Von Mumser holds a Sc.D., Doctor of Science in Chemistry, with a Masters in Chemistry. When he was in the military, besides the time he served overseas, he was stationed at Edgewood before the Gulf War. He worked as a biochemical warfare engineer at the Chemical Corp Laboratory in Edgewood, Maryland. He knows just about all there is about chemicals, toxins, and antidotes."

"Thanks, Jack that certainly gives me something to think about." Maris told him. Then to Stella she said, "Well Lady, I will keep trying and report back when I have some new results." With that Maris ended the call.

Stella told Jack, "Until we decide that we need to seek help from your boss, I would appreciate it if you did not mention this conversation to him. If Mr. Von Mumser does not talk about his skills, he may not want public awareness of his high educational degrees. He also might have personal issues with what he did in prior work assignments with chemicals that were meant to do harm and he now wants nothing to do with it. We will let you know before we have any talks with Von Mumser about his chemical knowledge. That way, you can approach him first and let us know how receptive he is to talking about toxins."

"Jack," Stella had him look her in the eye, "I need you to give me your word on this. I know how close you are with your boss, but I need your word not to reveal this talk." Jack was clearly uncomfortable, but he did agree.

It was about ten minutes later that Steve and Sal arrived with the security tapes. Jack was put in another room with Sal to review the tapes. He was given the same instructions as the personnel in Boston; to makes notes of anything unusual or out of place. Stella asked Steve to remain in the room.

After the others have left her office, she related to Steve what she learned from Jack earlier, to include Von Mumser's various degrees. "I want a very detailed background on Richard Von Mumser—ASAP! I want to know when he was at Edgewood. What projects did he work on? Who worked with him? And Steve, I need this information yesterday." She told him to use the research section in the building for today. She then told him that she wanted to see both him and Sal after Jack reviewed the tapes and was dismissed.

As Steve was about to leave the room to start his research, he turned to Stella and told her that he had checked it out and Massachusetts was the sixth state and Maryland was the seventh. He then gave her a two-fingered salute to his forehead and left the room.

It was several hours later when Jack had finished viewing all the tapes. Sal asked Jack if there was any significance in whether Von Mumser pulled a business card from his right or left jacket pocket. Jack explained to Sal that the cards in the Chairman's right pocket were give aways. The Chairman kept a list of local restaurants on cards in his left pocket. He would take out a card and ask if the place was any good and where it was located in relationship to the capitol building. He liked to ask the local residents about the restaurants to show an interest in the area where they lived. Those cards were not give-aways.

"Have you guys ever stayed long enough after an appearance to actually go to any of the restaurants?" Sal asked. "Sometimes," Jack told him, "if we were staying over night."

When they were ready to leave the viewing room, Sal told Jack to consider this viewing as confidential. They did not want Mr. Von Mumser to worry about what someone else may be doing to harm people and they did not want anyone else to misinterpret what was on the security tapes or their conversations. Sal then emphasized that if there was anything of value on the tapes, they did not want to give any heads up to the killer.

"And how am I not going to tell my boss about this office call when he knows where I am?" Jack asked.

"You can tell him that you were asked to view the tapes to see if you recognized any of the faces in the crowd—period. That is true, no lies there." Sal told him.

"Most important, Jack is that you remember that this is an investigation and we do not want to falsely upset or accuse anyone. We do not want to give away any inside information that might give the killer any warning, and even more dire, we do not want to give the victims' families any false hope. I am hoping to have your cooperation because we know how important Mr. Von Mumser is to you and the community. We also know that you want this solved so that any potential threat to him is eliminated.

Consider that if someone close to your boss is the source of these killings and you tell your boss about our investigations; he may unknowingly say something to this person. That might not bode well for your boss's safety."

Jack saw the logic in what Sal was saying and agreed to remain silent. But inwardly, he resolved to watch every member of the coalition committee for any suspicious activities. Whoever was targeting the Chairman had to be someone who knew him well, Jack reasoned. Then he thought that it could be just about any committee member. He knew that most of the committee members have known the Chairman for decades. Jack decided that he needed to be more alert to those people's actions. This was not a situation of employee loyalty, he rationalized.

This was because he knew, with every fiber of his being, what a good, caring person the Chairman was. Richard Von Mumser's life was dedicated to bettering the lives of others, not taking lives. Jack was in a hurry to have this maniac exposed.

Looking at Sal he asked if he could say goodbye to Stella before he left. Sal was aware that Jack was attracted to Stella. Heck, if he were twenty years younger he might have asked her out himself. She was the type of woman any man would be honored to just know and he felt lucky just being an associate. Sal bobbed his head a few times. "Sure, come on. Then I'll escort you out."

When Sal returned to Stella's office after seeing Jack out of the building, he felt they needed a little bit of humor. "Well, boss lady; it seems you have acquired another admirer. I wouldn't be surprised if you started getting a room full of flowers."

Stella gave him a blank look. "What are you talking about Sal?"

"The Chairman's aide, Jack Yu, he has a big case of puppy worship. Take it from me, Stella, as a guy, I can tell. He really likes you." Her only acknowledgement to that statement was "Umm." She changed the direction back to the business at hand.

"Steve, what were you able to find out about Mr. Von Mumser in the last few hours?"

"Well, he was born into money and privilege. He was an excellent student and does indeed hold a Sc.D, from Georgetown University and a Masters in Chemistry from Johns Hopkins. He was an officer in the DC National Guard, with the highest rank held of Major. While in the service, he was assigned to and worked on biochemical warfare agents for the Army's Chemical Corp Laboratory at Edgewood, Maryland.

I have requested a copy of his military file. That will tell us his assignments and the dates. I would like to talk with any of his previous military coworkers, if possible, to find out if there was any particular project that he was assigned to. Never know what you can learn when you turn a rock over.

Anyway, after active military duty in Kuwait, he went back to his reserve status and went to work with his father. After his father died, he founded the Coalition Committee for DC Statehood, of which he is the

Chairman. He and his wife belong to and work with many social and political organizations in the area. I would not want to accuse this man of something and be wrong. The influence he welds is tremendous." Steve then placed his research papers in front of Stella in case she wanted to re-read anything.

"I agree, we don't want to step on this man's toes," Stella commented. "I suggest that we keep on our course, but to do so discretely. Let me know what you come up with." Looking at the shadows under both men's eyes, she knew there was nothing more to be accomplished today. She told them that she wanted to meet again in a few days, after she had the reports from everyone in Massachusetts. Then they all left the building together.

Chapter XXV

February 15, 2015
Stella Vega's Office
FBI Building
Washington, DC

EARLY MORNING

Sitting in her office, Stella was reading Woods' report on his investigation of Richard Von Mumser. Steve had a list of names of people that were stationed at Edgewood at the same time as Von Mumser. Sal was doing a background on each one to see if maybe there were any old situations that may have festered into some type of revenge.

They were most interested in locating a Capt. Edward B. Smith. This man was Von Mumser's program partner on their biochemical projects. Capt. Smith left the military in the late eighties. He went back to Rhode Island, where he lived with his parents. But, inquiries there show that he moved away in the mid-nineties, after his parents died. They had not found any other relatives and no one there knew where he had relocated to. Since he was not in the military long enough to retire, there was no retirement check to trail. At this time they were waiting for information from the Social Security Administration on his current employment records.

Stella was surprised when she answered her phone to hear Maris Ayin's voice. "Stella, you will not believe what I have to tell you. Seems our little genius, Brandon Cohen, has unlocked another clue. He called me yesterday and I promised to pass on the information."

"Okay, okay. Maris you have me on the edge of my seat. Tell me what the young Mr. Cohen had to say."

"Seems he noticed that not only were the killings happening in the states in the order that they entering the Union, but also on the anniversary dates. With that information, it would seem that Maryland is to be the next target, on April 28th. If that is true, this kid is brilliant and I think you should talk to him about a future job."

"Yeah," Stella replied, "you're right. We can always use more hot shots. Thanks Maris. I'll check out Von Mumser's schedule to see if the dates marry up. I appreciate the tip."

After her talk with Maris, Stella placed a call to Jack Yu. He was happy to be of help. He confirmed that the Chairman is indeed scheduled to visit Maryland on April 28th. Of course, he told her, that was the current plan. He had no way to predict a postponement or a cancellation if the killer was still at large by then. Stella told Jack that she was going to do her best to bring this case to a close before them.

Then, as a thought came to her, she asked Jack if he had ever heard of a Capt. Edward B. Smith. Jack chuckled and told her that he not only knew of Capt. Smith, he saw him just a couple of days ago. Stella wondered how it was possible that the FBI had spent days tracking down a man who was not lost or hiding. She asked Jack where she could locate Capt. Smith. He told her that Capt. Edward B. Smith was Josh Von Mumser's godfather, Uncle Bennie. He further informed her that the B. in Edward B. Smith was for Benjamin. Uncle Bennie has worked with Josh Von Mumser for the last fifteen years.

Stella was delighted with the information and said so to Jack. "Does this mean that we will be having that cup of coffee soon?" Jack teased, hopefully.

"Close, Jack, but not yet," Stella replied. She thanked him again for the information and hung up.

Her next call was to Steve and Sal. She relayed what she had learned form Maris and Jack. She told them she was going to send someone out to Josh Von Mumser's office and request a talk with the former Capt. Smith for this afternoon. "Think you guys can be here by, say, three this afternoon?"

Steve gave a deep sigh. "Sure, we'll be there. Maybe, instead of all these back and forth trips, we should think about renting a monthly place. That would be lots cheaper than all these plane tickets."

"Sounds like a plan to me," Stella replied just a little too chipper for Steve's liking. "I'm sure I can get that cleared with my boss. Just let me know if that is what you two decide," she commented as she hung up.

Stella arranged for another member of the staff to go to Josh Von Mumser's firm, with a warrant, to bring the former Capt. Smith to her office at three. With that done, she had some time to compare Richard Von Mumser against her profile of the killer. With what she now knew about his background, it was amazing how easily she could fit him into her outline. She decided to hold her analysis to herself for the moment. She was eager to see what "Uncle" Bennie had to say.

MID-AFTERNOON

Steve and Sal arrived at two forty-five in the afternoon. The three of them were seated in Stella's office still debating whether the two men should rent an apartment in DC when Mr. Smith's arrival was announced.

When he entered the office, Stella was surprised how very opposite from Richard Von Mumser he appeared. She knew he was in his mid-fifties but he looked a bit younger. There was no grey in his sandy brown hair and he wore the latest frameless glasses. It made his blue eyes stand out. At five feet, nine inches he still had a youthful build and when he smiled, as he was doing now, it showed a dimple in each cheek. Stella rose from behind her desk and greeted the man. Then she introduced Steve and Sal. She indicated the chair across from her desk for Mr. Smith to use. Steve and Sal sat at the small round table off to the left of Stella's desk.

Stella opened the conversation. "Mr. Smith, I understand that you served in the military with Richard Von Mumser. That you were both stationed at the Army's Chemical Corp Laboratory at Edgewood, Maryland. I was wondering if you two worked on any special projects that involved biochemical products."

Bennie looked at her a few moments before responding. "Agent Vega, we were stationed at a Biochemical experimental facility. Of course we worked with biochemical products. May I ask what this is about? Has something happened to Richard? From something he worked with years ago?"

"No, no, nothing like that," she answered him. "Mr. Smith, you were in the military. So you will understand when I tell you that something is confidential. If I were to confide our investigation or suspicions to you, would you be able to assure me that you could keep it close hold?" Bennie sat up straighter in his chair and his face no longer held any hint of humor.

He was a display of grave seriousness when he said, "Lady, military training or not, I am a loyal American. If there is something you need from me, just tell me. If there is something you need me to do, just tell me. Cat-and-mouse is not my style of doing business. So why don't you just cut to the chase and we can move on from there?"

Steve and Sal remained silent, letting Stella decide their course of action. "Okay, Mr. Smith, I agree with you," Stella told him. "I was, and am, only concerned with your close friendship with Richard Von Mumser. It seems that death has been trailing his state visits. Neither the CDC nor the EPA can isolate the culprit causing these deaths. Based on information that has recently come to our attention, we believe your friend and former military lab worker may be a suspect." She paused to look directly into Bennie's eyes. At first there was nothing. Then she saw confusion and doubt.

"Wait a minute," he said. "Are you saying that Dick is responsible? That he has been committing these murders? How is that possible? He was out there for the whole world to see? I've been following these articles. I can't say for certain, but I doubt he even knew all those people who died. That would be too weird."

"Mr. Smith," Steve spoke up, "I know this is a shock for you. But let me explain how we came to this point." Steve went on to explain to Bennie about the toxicology reports, the videos and photographs of Von Mumser only using his left pocket cards when in contact with the victims and his advanced knowledge of chemical engineering. "What we want to know from you is if, during your research time together, did Mr. Von Mumser say or do anything that would indicate a fascination with any particular undetectable chemicals. I realize that that was your job. But I'm talking about something that might go beyond the job. Something he had a personal interest in. Something that the world outside of your research lab would not have known anything about."

Bennie did not say anything for several minutes as he just sat there and looked at each person. As if making up his mind, he nodded once and spoke. "I seem to recall that Richard was particularly fascinated with a chemical named Phosgene Oxime. This toxin is no longer manufactured as its use on the battlefield was never favorable documented. While it is possible that some storage of this chemical may actually still exist, officially, it is extinct. Richard thought that he could improve on the chemical's properties to eliminate its disagreeable penetrating odor and make it more fact acting. As it was then, it took from two to six days, with the right amount of exposure, to be fatal. I have no idea if he ever achieved his goal."

Bennie appeared to think over what he had just said and told the agents, "If this turns out to be a man I have known for more than half of my life, a man I consider to be like a brother, I am going to be crushed. Yet, at the same time, should you be correct, then that proves the theory that you never really know someone. What a sad state of affairs. Do you have any idea why Dick would do such a thing?"

"Who knows why anyone decides to step over the line," Sal commented. "Mr. Smith, we appreciate your cooperation and candor. Please remember that we are asking you to treat this conversation with strict confidentiality. We request that you do not discuss this with anyone outside of this room. Particularly with your godson. Should this prove baseless, then you can pretend that this talk never happened and no one will be affected."

"Yes, I agree," Bennie stated. "I do ask that you please let me know what you find. I don't want to have to look at my friend and wonder about his stability if he is not involved."

"We can do that," Stella said. "Mr. Smith, thank you again for coming here today. Agent Woods will return you to your office." As an added thought, she asked, "Is Mr. Josh Von Mumser at work today? I mean, would he be there when you return?"

Bennie looked directly at Stella. "Agent Vega, I told you I would not reveal a word of our meeting. I'm not pleased that you are already questioning my word."

"Oh no sir," she replied. "That was not my intention, nor the reason for the question. While Agent Woods takes you back, I was going to have him bring Mr. Von Mumser in for a similar chat. We would not mention your visit here in any conversation we might have with Mr. Von Mumser."

"Oh, I see," Bennie said. "Sorry for the misunderstanding. Yes, Josh usually stays at work until eight in the evening. Unless he has an evening engagement, which I would not know about. But he came in today." Bennie paused at this point to fully gain Stella's attention. "Agent Vega, I don't know how much you know about Josh's relationship with his father. In fact, they really don't have one. I think the term would be estranged. I'm not sure he could help you very much."

"Thank you Mr. Smith. But Agents Woods and Caruso have, in fact, already had a talk with Mr. Von Mumser. But now we just need to dig a bit deeper." Turning to Steve, she told him to escort Mr. Smith back to his office and to bring Mr. Von Mumser back to her office. She walked them both to the office door to see them out.

Closing the door, she went back to her desk and sat down. "Okay Sal, while Steve is picking up the young Mr. Von Mumser, I need you to do some research. I want to know everything available about this…" here she referred to a note she made, "…Phosgene Oxime. I suggest you start with Maris Ayin and her sources. While you're doing that, I'm going to check out some military biochemical records. I figure with the Northern Virginia rush hour, Steve should be back here at about six o'clock. We'll plan to regroup here at that time. Okay?"

"Sure, boss lady. But first tell me where you hide the vending machines in this building. I ain't had no lunch and I hate it when my stomach talks louder than my brain." Stella laughed and gave him the directions.

EARLY EVENING

Josh Von Mumser entered Stella's office with an air of confidence. He had nothing to hide and was ready to answer any questions. He knew when Steve approached him earlier that the visit would have to do with his father. While he rarely thought or spoke about the man, he was ready to cooperate with the authorities.

Josh was given the chair that Bennie had occupied a few hours earlier. "Mr. Von Mumser," Stella began. "I understand that your father holds a Doctorate of Science in Chemistry."

"Yes ma'am, he does," Josh replied. He then hurried on before anything more could be said. "If no one here has any objection, I really would prefer to be addressed as Josh. Mr. Von Mumser is my father. I am Josh."

"Okay, Josh, fine by me," Sal told him and continued on. "Do you know if your father continued to work with any chemical research projects after he left the military?"

"By that, do you mean, does he play at being a mad scientist? If so, I can only tell you that he considered chemistry a pastime, a hobby. At least that was what he said when I was still living at home. He had a real elaborate laboratory in the basement, where he spent hours. Since I haven't been down there in years, I don't even know if it is still there. Is there a reason to know?"

"Let me ask you this," Sal replied. "Do you recall your father ever mentioning a substance called Phosgene Oxime?"

"No, can't say that I have. What is it?" Josh asked.

"Was," Sal said. "It was an experimental biochemical warfare agent that the military stopped working with in the eighties. Your father was the lead researcher. Supposedly the entire agent was destroyed. But, we have reason to believe that maybe your father never gave up his research with this toxin."

"Well, what can I do to help you?" Josh asked. "I never heard of this substance and have no way of knowing what my father did, or does, in the basement."

"Sir," Steve said, "We need to see if his laboratory still exists and if so, what he is working on. Short of barging into the house, do you know of a way for us to check? If there is nothing there, we don't want a big brouhaha in the press about harassing the man."

"Oh, I see, some undercover work, huh?" Josh stated. "Well, I know that search warrants are no strangers to you; having been served myself with one recently. So why don't you get one of those handy dandy pieces of paper and use it next week when my parents are out of town. They are going to Florida for a few days to visit with my sister and her family. The house will be empty. I still have a key, at my mother's insistence, and can let you in.

But I'll warn you in advance. If my father does still work in his lab, he will know in an instant if anything has been touched or moved. He was very meticulous about his research."

"Got it," Sal said. "Thanks for the heads up. We'll work out the details and let you know when to meet us at the house. We ask that you not discuss this with anyone; not your wife and most importantly, not your mother. I don't see any need to raise emotions if nothing is there." As an added comment, Sal said, "And you can tell the Dragon Lady, err, I mean Kate, that you are meeting some buddies to cover any time away from the office."

Josh's eyebrows rose a little at Sal's comment. "Dragon Lady, huh? I guess she can seem that way to people who don't know her. I like her efficiency and no-nonsense. But, maybe Dragon Lady is a way to describe her," he finished with a smile. Josh told them he understood what they expected from him and would cooperate. He would wait for their call. He gave them the dates that his parents would be out of town and rose to leave the office.

As Steve was leaving to take Josh back to his office, Stella told him to meet her and Sal at Chef Theo's in White Oak, their usual eating place when the men were in town, at about eight-thirty. "Can do, boss lady. If you get there before me, order me the lamb chops, medium rare. See you soon," he said as he closed the office door.

Chapter XXVI

February 24, 2015
Richard Von Mumser's Home
Washington, DC

As Josh Von Mumser pulled into the curved driveway he saw the sedan with government plates already parked by the carriage house. Four people got out of the vehicle as he turned off his engine. Josh recognized Agents Vega, Woods and Caruso, but he had not met the other woman with them. She was carrying what looked like a large metal cooler.

By the time he had gotten out of his car, the others had reached him. Stella introduced the new member of her group. "Mr. Josh Von Mumser, this is Superintendent Maris Ayin, from the Atlanta CDC. She is the one who will actually be inspecting any chemicals that we may come across."

Josh shook hands with Maris but did not comment. To Stella he said, "Okay, I'm sure you have your warrant, so let's get this started."

He shifted the keys on his key ring until he found the one he needed to unlock the house. "Let me enter first," he told them. "I have to disarm the security system. Mother told me she would never let my father change the code so that both my sister and I would always be welcome. I never thought I would actually ever use it again." The four waited at the front entrance while Josh went inside. He was back in mere seconds and let them into the house.

It was an elegant Georgian style home with high ceilings and elaborate cherry cross molding where the walls met the ceiling. It did not look so large from the outside. The furniture was straight out of

Southern Living with highly polished hardwood floors, silk and satin cushioned furniture, exquisite brocade drapes, faux gaslights on the walls accentuated with a fifteen foot long hanging crystal chandelier in the foyer. There was a wide central staircase facing the entrance that branched out at the top of the stairs to form a balcony around the upper level that overlooked the main floor. Stella had the impression of either stepping back into history, or into a museum, as she looked around at the ancestral portraits, the antiques, the crystal, and the china on display.

Josh was moving ahead into the interior of the house. When he came to a restaurant size kitchen, he opened a door next to another set of stairs that led to the floor above. The door that he opened was the passageway down into the basement. Josh turned on the lights and they all descended the steps. The basement was as majestic as the floor above. This area was entirely lined with cedar. The area that took up the entire right half of the room was devoted to wines and what looked like old and expensive liqueurs. To the immediate left of the stairway was a very modern laundry room, complete with a laundry chute from the floors above. The back left area appeared to be a storage area with crates, luggage, and boxes.

"Nice tour, Josh," Sal said. "But I don't see no laboratory."

"That's because it is not in the main area. Look around and you can see that this space does not cover the house space above. The laboratory is on the other side of that wall." Josh pointed to the wall between the laundry room and the storage area. "When my father modernized the laundry area, he walled off the remainder of the basement area for his own use," Josh told the others as he walked toward the door that they could now see. It blended well into the wall.

When Josh opened the door, it led them into a very well equipped research facility, quality laboratory. There were microscopes, a freezer unit, Bunsen burners, jars, glass slides, and all manners of containers with various colors and types of liquids and chemicals, and a variety of other scientific equipment. It was at this point that Maris told the others to leave the room. She wanted to search the area herself. In the event that she discovered something lethal, she did not want anyone to be exposed.

Stella agreed that that was a good precaution and that, with Steve and Sal, they would use the time to search the rest of the house for any other potential evidence. She told Maris to take her time and that they would be back after looking through the house. Maris agreed and waited for them to leave the room. Then, as she was closing the door, she heard Stella ask Josh, "Please show us which one is your parents' bedroom."

Left alone, Maris quickly donned a portable plastic jumpsuit with full safety headgear and gloves. She meticulously moved from one area to another in the room. She was able to identify the majority of each vial and liquid she saw. She was very glad that Von Mumser was a neat freak and he had labeled just about everything.

When she opened the top left hand drawer of Von Mumser's desk she found a small plastic zippered case that contained two vials. One was an atomizer and the other was a clear liquid with a screw on cap. Neither vial was labeled. She took two small samples from the liquid vial, placed each in a separate glass container, and placed those in her metal cooler. From the atomizer, she took two small sprays on cloth and placed each cloth in a glass container and also placed them in her metal container. She continued her search of the room and its contents. Her search completed, Maris removed the protective wear and placed them in a plastic lined disposable laundry bag that she had brought with her. She was anxious to return to Atlanta to begin her analyses.

When she came out of the room, the others were waiting for her. "Well, I hope your search was as fruitful as mine may be," she commented as she help up her metal cooler.

"Oh, yeah, I think we were," Sal told her as he held up a plastic evidence bag. He then told Maris how they searched Richard Von Mumser's bedroom, a separate room from Mrs. Von Mumser's, and they discovered an added feature in all of his suit coats and sports jackets. All the outside pockets were fitted to accommodate Velcro held plastic liners. There were several dozen pairs of liners in a drawer in the armoire. There was also one pair of liners still inside one sports coat.

That was the pair in the evidence bag. Sal had used one of the unused pairs to replace the pair now held in the bag. Maris asked if she could have the liners to analyze along with the evidence that she had collected. Sal was glad to turn it over to her.

Overall they were in the house less than two hours. When they left, Josh reset the security system and walked with the four others to his car. Stella thanked him again for his assistance and reminded him of the strict confidentiality regarding their investigation. He nodded his understanding and told them that he hoped they were able to find what they needed.

Josh remained in the driveway as he watched their sedan pull out onto the main street. Then, as he got back into his car, he thought that maybe this would be the blessing in disguise that his mother needed to be released from his father's tight fisted control.

Chapter XXVII

March 6, 2015
Atlanta, Georgia and Washington, DC

Maris Ayin's Office
Atlanta, Georgia

The analyses were finished on the samples she had taken from Von Mumser's house. There was nothing to be found on the pocket liners. Obviously, they were newly placed in the pockets as they still had manufacturer's powder on the inside. But the vials were an entirely different situation. She now had some interesting news to report. When she dialed Stella's number it was answered on the second ring. Stella must have recognized Maris' number on her telephone's Caller ID because of the way she answered. "Maris, how are you? How did you know that I had been thinking about you? Are you calling with some new information?"

Maris could not wait to give her report. "Stella, I hope that you are sitting down because you are going to be one happy lady. I have in my hand the analyses from those samples we collected and you were right, this stuff is absolutely fascinating."

Stella could not remain silent and just cut in on Maris. "Oh, please, please, please just tell me we have that defunked warfare agent…. Phos….Phos….whatever."

Maris gave a small chuckle and pronounced it for her. "Phos-gene Ox-ime. Or, if you prefer the Latin name, Oxima De Fosgeno. Relax girl, sit back and let me report, okay?"

"Okay, just don't forget to report in people-speak so that I will be able to understand everything," Stella told her.

"Got it," Maris replied. "Well, from the tests we performed and the information available through the military on the prior properties of this warfare agent, I would say that our guy has been very busy. And I will add that he sure seems to know his stuff. The potency of the Phosgene Oxime in the atomizer is some fifty times that of when the military was testing it. It also has no discernible odor, is absorbed through the skin, and can cause pulmonary arrest in thirty minutes to two hours, without leaving an outward trace, because the chemical evaporates when exposed to the air. The original time span was estimated to be six hours to two days. We are talking major acceleration here girlfriend.

The clear liquid appears to be the antidote. So, if our killer is Von Mumser and he takes the antidote before descending into the public visitors' area, he is safe. However, with the chemical evaporating when exposed to the air, he must have a way to keep his supply throughout the day. I would say that this explains the plastic lined coat pockets. If the liner is coated with the spray version, any card taken out gets renewed when put back into the pocket.

So, now that we know the how and with what, what are we going to do about it? Do we just go up and arrest the bastard?"

Stella gave an immediate No. "It is going to be vital to catch him in the act. But, we need to make sure that not one more life is at risk. Maris, you saw the containers that the samples came from. Do you think you can create placebos for both vials? In both appearance and design? And in containers identical to those you saw?"

"Stella, I am so motivated to get this guy I could duplicate Colonel Sander's secret fried chicken recipe. However, it is always a snap to say you can do something and then it actually takes two snaps to get it done. To be realistic, I'm going to say that it may take me a few weeks to get it done. Will that be soon enough? If not, maybe I could get a few extra people on the project to work in shifts."

"No, Maris, a few weeks will be plenty of time to make the fakes. With the information we have on Von Mumser's schedule, we have about six weeks before our guy will try anything else. In the meantime, we have to get our ducks in order and be more than one hundred percent ready for his next state road show." Maris heard the sigh Stella expended before she spoke again.

"Maris you know that I am thrilled that we have been able to uncover the method and the probable culprit. I am just sorry that it ended up being a man who obviously did so much good and is someone that so many people admire. But, he isn't, and won't be, someone who commits mayhem and thinks that his position will protect him."

Maris, who was dedicated to the prevention of disease and illness, could not find it in herself to sympathize with Stella. "Oh, you mean like Hitler or Saddam Hussein? Sorry lady, he gets no bonus points from me if he has intentionally set out to harm even one person. I'm going to get working on those placebos today. I'll call you back when it's done. And Stella," Maris added, "Don't let the bad guys get you down. Talk to you soon," she concluded and ended the call.

Stella Vega's Office
Washington, DC

Stella sat at her desk contemplating the sharp turn in events. She was glad that they were closing in on this killer. Yet, she was still puzzled over the motive. No matter how she looked at it, she could not understand what made Von Mumser turn to murder. Surely, he could see that this would not aid his cause in any way, so the question came back to the basic one—Why?

She had to telephone Steve and Sal to tell them of the results of Maris' tests and the plan to develop placebos. While she was dialing the number, she thought that it was a good thing the guys had decided not to stay in the Washington area for the remainder of the case. It seemed that their presence here would not be needed for awhile. Both men were in their New York office and placed her on the speaker. When Stella have finished relating the latest information, they told her how pleased they were with the report and told Stella it was almost time to congratulate themselves. But, they would postpone the festivities until after the final act.

Stella asked them to contact Josh Von Mumser and Bennie Smith, as promised. She decided that they were not going to say anything to either Jack Yu or Julius Walsh. At least not at this time. She also told Steve and Sal that they had to wait for Maris to come up with the fakes. Then they were going to pay a visit to the governor of Maryland.

When Steve asked her what she was going to do while they were put on hold, she told them. She had promised Governor Matsangakis that she would report any developments and that is what she was going to do. She was not going to reveal any identities yet as she did not want to risk any leaks to make Von Mumser suspect anything. But, she did plan to make a personal trip to Boston.

Steve and Sal understood her position. Having to tell someone that while you were able to solve a murder, this was a good thing; having to tell them that if a little more information had been available the deaths could have been prevented, was not good from any angle. They wished her luck and hung up.

Stella continued to sit at her desk for a long while before making another call. This one was to Boston. Andreas answered the governor's phone. After listening to her request for personal time with Matsangakis, Andreas told her she could see the governor tomorrow afternoon. She thanked him, hung up, and then made a call to place an airline reservation. She knew tomorrow was going to be one long day.

Chapter XXVIII

April 4, 2015
Governor's Office
Annapolis, Maryland

Armed with the information that Maris had successfully developed the placebos, Stella, Steve, and Sal were about to present their plan to the Maryland Governor, F. Stephen Michaels. Their appointment was for ten in the morning. At exactly five minutes to ten, the governor's executive assistant, A. Phillip Leder, escorted them into the governor's private office. Knowing his boss as well as he did, Leder told the governor that coffee was on the way and left the agents to introduce themselves.

Seated at his desk, Governor Michaels rose to meet his guests. He nodded at Leder's comment and waited until the office door was closed. Stella, who watched the governor come in their direction, got positive vibrations from the man's appearance. Stella wondered what secret credo top politicians worked under. It seemed to her that all the governors that she had encountered recently did not present the stereotypical image of the kind, elderly statesman. More like health conscience energetic individuals.

Governor Michaels was a man in his sixties but clearly did not look his age. At five feet eleven inches, he had a solid athletic build that did not reflect any "love handles". His hair, though thinning, retained a large amount of its youthful dark brown. Most impressive to Stella was the absence of facial lines. "I wonder if he uses a face cream," she thought, "and if he would be willing to share his secret." His dark eyes looked almost chocolate in color and intelligent, like he was taking in everyone and everything. He also moved in a calm, relaxed, self assured manner.

Stella moved forward to meet the man halfway. She performed the required introductions and told the governor that they were there to ask his assistance. The governor waived them over to a small, square, table in the corner of his office near the tall bay windows that overlooked the capitol grounds. As Sal watched Stella make the introductions he had the thought that he would never be able to work for the State of Maryland. "Everyone we have met so far has a first name initial. I ain't got no middle name, so they probably wouldn't even look at my resume."

Once everyone was seated, Stella began the meeting. "Governor Michaels, I am sure you are aware of the deaths that have occurred in the past few months in nearby state capitols." She paused expecting some sort of acknowledgement from the governor.

Instead of merely nodding, Michaels spoke up. "Yes, I am very aware of the murders and what appears to be the catalyst for them…visits from the DC Coalition Chairman, Richard Von Mumser. Agent Vega, I know what you are about to ask of me. The same thing you asked of my friend and colleague, Pierre Matsangakis. I must tell you up front that I can not and will not risk the life of even one person to repeat the situation that occurred in Boston." The determination of his position came across loud and clear without him having raised his voice.

"Governor Michaels," Stella replied. "Please hear us out before you make that final decision." Her respect for the man increased when he nodded his okay for her to continue. At that moment, Leder rapped on the door and entered rolling in a tea cart with coffee, tea, and small pastries. They did not resume their talk until everyone had gotten a drink and a pastry and returned to the table. Leder left the room with instructions from the governor not to allow any interruptions.

Stella proceeded to inform Michaels about their investigation and discoveries. She told him about the chemical they found in Von Mumser's house and Maris' ability to make the placebos. Steve and Sal laid out their plans on how they intended to catch Von Mumser in action. Only this time, not one single person would be in danger because he would be using placebos without knowing it. When Stella could see that they had not fully convinced the governor to help them, she played what she considered a trump card.

"Governor Michaels, have you considered what a win for justice this would be? Mr. Von Mumser acquired the supplies for this poison while stationed in the military at Edgewood, a facility in Maryland. This substance was a toxin developed specifically for use in time of war as a dirty bomb with only one intent, death. Supposedly this toxin was destroyed and disposed of on Maryland land at either the Aberdeen or Edgewood property. Something that we now know was not completely accomplished.

Yes, I know that those installations are Federal property. But they reside within the Maryland borders. It would be so right for this man to be taken into custody in Maryland. Sort of a case of just desserts. Plus, with what you now know, we would leave it to you to call the EPA, or OSHA, to come in and re-inspect the records and grounds at Edgewood. Of course, that action could only be viewed as your dedication for the health and safety of the people in Maryland."

Michaels saw what she was doing. She was putting him in a position to either cooperate and come out a hero, or, decline and maybe put other lives at stake. As was expected, he opted for cooperation. Once that decision was made, he wanted to know what they needed from him and exactly how they planned to carry out the arrest. He asked for assurances, several times, that absolutely no one would be in danger.

Stella explained that it was most important that the original meeting take place as planned, with one change. Seeing as how the date of the meeting coincided with the anniversary of Maryland's statehood, she knew that the governor had a state government breakfast planned. She wanted Michaels to invite Von Mumser and his wife to a small dinner party the night before. Just eight or ten people. And Michaels was to provide the Von Mumsers with a room in the governor's mansion. While the dinner was in progress, her team would make the switch to the placebos. That way, if Von Mumser thinks to prepare himself before he leaves his room in the morning, there will be no chance of danger.

Then, in the morning Von Mumser and his assistant would attend the breakfast. Mrs. Von Mumser would remain at the mansion for a brunch with Mrs. Michaels and await her husband's return. This plan ensured that Von Mumser and Jack Yu were occupied. In addition, the DC Daily reporter that chronicled Von Mumser's campaign would be where the Chairman was.

For her part, Stella informed Michaels, she would convince Von Mumser that he would have the same level of security that he had in Massachusetts, maybe even more intense. This way he could continue his planned visit without any added worry.

While Michaels wanted assurances from Stella, she asked for one of her own. "Sir, do you think you will be able to carry this off? Will you be able to act in your normal manner without giving anything away when you are face-to-face with Von Mumser?"

"Agent Vega, I am the Governor of Maryland and, I'd like to think, a consummate politician. If nothing else, I have learned how to **not** reveal my inner feelings. You will have no problem with me. I will issue the invitations in a few days. But first I have to "arrange" the dinner party with my wife."

As an after thought, Michaels asked her, "However, have you given any thought to the possibility that Von Mumser might decline the dinner invite, that he might have other plans?"

"Yes sir, that thought had crossed my mind." Then she looked Michaels directly in the eye, smiled, and said, "But sir, you are such a consummate politician, I have full faith that you can convince him to change his plans and attend your function."

Taken off guard, Michaels chuckled and replied, "Touché, Agent Vega, touché."

The four of them spoke a little longer hammering out the details of the impending arrest of Von Mumser. When Michaels was convinced he had all the details he offered to take them to lunch at a local Fish-&-Chips bar in Old Town Annapolis. The agents accepted the offer and followed Michaels out of his office.

Chapter XXIX

April 28, 2015
State Capitol Building
Annapolis, Maryland

    The Maryland Delegation Breakfast went off as planned with Von Mumser and Yu as guests. Sal thought it was almost as smooth as their search of Von Mumser's suite last night, minus any of the political speeches. He recalled how pleased Maris Ayin had been to cooperate. They had used a back entrance that was under their security control to let Maris in. Then Stella took her to the Von Mumser rooms and stood watch in the hallway while Maris searched inside.
    Maris was totally prepared with her portable chemical protective clothing. After switching the vials, she left the mansion taking the hermetically sealed real vials to the local CDC containment office.
    Stella was able to give the thumbs up to Governor Michaels after Maris' departure. It seemed to Stella that Michaels visibly relaxed when he knew all was going as planned.
    Following the breakfast, Stella and Sal escorted Von Mumser, Jack and Julius to Governor Michaels' reception area. Steve was given another task that prevented him from being at the actual meeting between Michaels and Von Mumser. But he was going to be center stage for the arrest. His job was to escort Mrs. Von Mumser to the capitol building when he got the call from Stella.
    Governor Michaels gave everyone a warm welcome, and then invited Von Mumser to join him in his private office. Stella, Sal, Jack and Julius passed the wait exchanging pleasantries with Michaels' executive assistant, Leder. For appearances, Stella and Sal made small

talk about security measures. Julius asked if there had been any progress with their investigations into who might be doing the killings. Sal, who had just taken a sip of coffee started to cough. Stella rushed over to pat Sal on the back then gave him a stern look.

Turning back to face Julius she reiterated her promise that when that information was available for public release he would have the exclusive story seeing how he had been so cooperative. Julius beamed, thinking he was helping the FBI to capture the slug that was trying to cast doubt on Von Mumser.

Twenty minutes after entering the private office, the door opened and both men came out. Michaels shook everyone's hand as they left to go downstairs. Stella was the last to leave and he held her hand longer and looked into her eyes. She gave a slight nod and then he released her hand.

Von Mumser and his group went out into the visitors' area and he started his usual routine of handing out leaflets and conversing with the visitors. One undercover agent, a young white male, approached Von Mumser and answered all the questions correctly. When Von Mumser made to reach into his left coat pocket for a card, the agent displayed his badge and asked the Chairman to quietly accompany him to a private area in the building.

Von Mumser was surprised that the authorities have zeroed in on him at this point and tried to bluff his way out. The agent informed him that he did not mind causing a scene, but he was well aware of Von Mumser's penchant for perfect public appearances. The Chairman went with him to a private office that had no windows. When he entered the office, he saw that Stella and Sal were already there. Stella explained that they knew what he had been doing and how. Von Mumser denied everything at this point.

The door to the private office opened and Steve escorted Mrs. Von Mumser into the room. Von Mumser asked what his wife was doing there. Steve told him that she asked to be here when she heard about the pending detainment.

Still feigning ignorance, Von Mumser denied any knowledge of any wrong doing. "Fine," Steve told him, "You just stay with that line. In the meantime, we will have to search your person." Steve then pulled on a pair of blue biochemical resistant gloves. He also asked another agent in the room to list the property he removed from Von Mumser.

Steve placed his gloved hand into Von Mumser's left coat pocket, closely watching Von Mumser's face for any reaction. There was no emotion, just a stoic expression. Steve commented on the oddity of finding the pocket plastic lined. Von Mumser did not reply. When Steve removed the business cards from the pocket he looked at them a moment before telling Mrs. Von Mumser that she could have them as her husband would not be needing them at this time.

As Steve moved to give her the cards and she extended one hand, palm up to receive the cards, which was when Von Mumser cracked. He knocked the cards out of Steve's hand and yelled at his wife not to touch them. Then he looked around the room and told everyone there not to touch the cards. Then he sagged into a nearby chair.

It seemed that despite everything, Richard Von Mumser did love his wife. He looked up at Steve and said that he was ready to talk.

"Talk?" Steve asked him. "About what?"

"About how I am responsible. I am the one that you have been looking for lately. I am the one that saw the validity .in utilizing those men as an example of the need for DC statehood."

"Sounds reasonable to me," Steve replied and looked over at Sal with a facial expression that plainly read light's on but nobody's home. "But don't say another word at this point." Looking around the room Steve saw an agent he had worked with in the past, Danny Rosenthal. Steve called to Rosenthal to come read Mr. Von Mumser his rights. Then Steve thought he might never have this chance again, and with a smile said, "Oh, by the way Agent Rosenthal, after you have informed Mr. Von Mumser of his Miranda rights; Book Him, Dano."

Chapter XXX

April 28, 2015
FBI Building
Washington, DC

The room being used for the interrogation was full to over flowing with representation from the major jurisdictions involved plus the accused part and his attorney.

Seated down one side of the oblong eight person conference table was Stella Vega in the center seat flanked on either side by her FBI team members, Steve Woods and Sal Caruso. Across the table in the center position was the accused, Richard Von Mumser, who was flanked by his lawyer, John Pugh, and his wife, Sandra, whom Richard insisted be with him. At one end of the table was Maris Ayin from the CDC. At the other end was an FBI stenographer, recording the entire process.

In addition, standing watch at the doorway was a member of the DC Capitol Police and the Maryland Capitol Police. Outside in the hallway, the entrance to the conference room was guarded by two uniformed security personnel.

Seated on the wooden bench outside the room were two people who had been denied admittance to the interrogation. One was Jack Yu, still believing there must be some mistake in the charges levied against his boss. The other person was the DC Daily reporter, Julius Walsh. While Jack was there in a show of support and faith in his boss; Julius, on the other hand had another objective. While greatly surprised by the arrest of Von Mumser, Julius was determined to have the breaking story for his paper.

In the conference room Von Mumser's attorney was stating his position as legal council for the accused. Pugh informed everyone that he had advised his client not to answer any questions nor make any statements without legal consent. "We also need to know exactly what charge Mr. Von Mumser is being accused of." Pugh continued. "Yes, I know that my client admitted having knowledge of a potential lethal poison that may, or may not, be connected with the victims at some state capitols. However, as my client had not been read his rights at the time of that conversation, anything he said cannot be used in a court of law against him."

"Actually, Mr. Pugh," Steve replied, "Your client was not under address at the time of that conversation, which he made in a public forum, and therefore no reading of his rights were required at that time. And, your client was read his rights at the time of his arrest. This, by the way, is how your name came up and how you came to be here now." Steve paused for that statement to settle on the lawyer.

"Now that we have cleared up that matter, I can tell you that Mr. Von Mumser is being charged with twenty-one counts of premeditated murder in six jurisdictions; one count of first degree murder in one jurisdiction; manufacture, transportation, and use of an illegal lethal chemical substance; theft of government property, false representation of a gubernatorial organization for personal gain, and improper use of numerous government buildings for immoral purposes. I haven't decided yet whether to pursue a charge of illegal use of his coalition position for personal gain. But if I do, I'm sure that his tax returns would not stand up well if his trips to any of these locations were listed as a business expense." From the tone of his voice Sal knew that Steve was clearly agitated with having to play legal ping pong with Von Mumser's council.

Steve returned to his original agenda. "Folks, if we are finished with all the required opening salvos, I would like to get this interrogation underway." When he looked around the table the slight nod that Von Mumser gave his attorney did not escape Steve's eyes. The only person there that earned any sympathy points from him was Mrs. Von Mumser who looked like she was going to melt into the floor from...from?...shock?...embarrassment?...disbelief?...disappointment?

Any one or all of those emotions were reflected in her red-rimmed, glassy-eyed stare that she kept on a spot on the wall behind Stella's head. She also maintained a death grip on her husband's left hand, which he returned. Steve focused his attention on the accused.

"Mr. Von Mumser, you are a very well known individual, influential in political circles, financially stable, a family man, well educated, an active member of numerous charity organizations, chairman of a powerful coalition, a pillar of the community, and even a role model to younger people. So, you can understand my not comprehending your actions of the past several months. I would like to know why. Why were you out there seemingly taking lives, at random, of innocent individuals? Yes, I believe that we should begin with that question, why?"

Steve paused, still locking gazes with Von Mumser, he saw Pugh shift in his chair as if in preparation for a protest. Before he could acknowledge the lawyer and prep for more legal jargon, Von Mumser put his free hand on Pugh's left forearm. "John," Von Mumser began, in a rather soft, tired sounding voice, "I appreciate what you are trying to do, I really do. But it's over. I am guilty of all those crimes mentioned earlier." Then pausing, he looked from his lawyer to his wife.

"Sandra, never doubt my love for you. I never understood what I ever did to earn a treasure like you. And now, because of a dream gone nightmare, you will be made the scapegoat for my sins. I am so sorry to be such a burden to you."

Sandra took her eyes off the far wall and looked at her husband. Mad though she knew him to be, she also knew that he loved her on some level. How sad that that level fell somewhere beneath his love of his dream. She managed a small smile, squeezed his hand once, and whispered, "Richard, I love you too. I cannot say that everything is going to be okay, because we both know that will not be. But I can tell you that I will not suffer. So don't waste your time with those thoughts. Let's just concentrate on what we can do to help you to get through this ordeal, okay?" Von Mumser gave her a smile and a nod of his head.

Returning his gaze to Steve, he said, "How can I help you? I know you have a lot of questions and I will answer them if I can. I know that my lawyer does not agree with me and has advised me not to say anything. But, I disagree with John and requested he be with me to ensure that my Constitutional rights are not violated, nothing more.

I must tell you in advance that I believe I was justified in all I did. I apologize if I have caused anyone pain, but they should be proud that those who died did so for a greater cause."

When he said no more, Steve placed his hands flat on the table and leaned across the space and spoke in a very strong voice. "What cause? What cause is so great that it can justify taking the lives of innocent bystanders, just because they had the misfortune to cross your path? Tell me; help me to understand this cause." Steve remained in his stance for several seconds as he fused his eyes with Von Mumser's. After a few more heartbeats he eased back and sat down.

Pugh was speaking even before Steve was fully in his chair. "You see, this is exactly what I was concerned about. It appears to me that Agent Woods is very emotional about this case and possibly cannot be objective in his questioning."

Stella's hand on Steve's arm told him not to reply. Without moving either towards the attorney or further back into her seat, she spoke to Pugh in a voice dripping with authority. "Mr. Pugh, Steve's emotional level, and his display, or not, of any emotional extremes, is solely my responsibility, thank you. And, as you yourself know, those we are responsible for don't always say or act as we would advise them to do."

Her point that Von Mumser, himself, was definitely acting against council by offering assistance was not lost on Pugh. "However, I need to add that I saw no objectionable behavior in either word or deed from Agent Woods. And mine is the decision that counts." She shifted her attention back to Woods. "Steve, please continue with your questions." While continuing to speak to Steve, she looked at Pugh, "And while I personally appreciate it, you may want to tone down the enthusiasm just a notch, okay?"

Steve took a deep breath and nodded. Looking back at Von Mumser he began anew. "Mr. Von Mumser, would you be so kind as to enlighten me, us, on this cause you mentioned earlier?"

"Certainly," Von Mumser stated. "The cause is, quite simply, one goal, statehood. Statehood for the people of the District of Columbia. A right and status long denied a whole segment of the American population. It is a travesty that because someone lives in the Capitol of the greatest country on earth that person cannot claim statehood, cannot claim that sanctity of being a state citizen."

Seeing that Von Mumser was gearing up for a campaign lecture, Steve cut into the rhetoric. "Okay, okay, I understand your interpretation of the cause. But you, as an active advocate for statehood, were doing everything politically possible, and legal, to obtain that goal. So, again I ask, why? Why did you decide to change your venue and attack not those in positions to assist you, but rather innocent bystanders?"

In response, Von Mumser stated, "That's just it, don't you see? They were not innocent bystanders. None of them."

Steve shot back, "Even if that were true, what about Ms. Villareal?"

"Who?" Von Mumser asked, with a confused look on his face.

"Ms. Gidget Villareal, the young woman, the only woman, the young black woman, who died in Connecticut. What was her part in your cause?"

"Oh, yes, her. I am really sorry about that. She was an unfortunate encounter that should not have happened. It was her own fault, you know. I told her not to help, that I could gather the papers myself. But would she listen? No. She just had to be the Good Samaritan. If she had listened to me, she would be alive today. And look where that good deed got her. I tried to ease her parents' pain, you know. I sent them a very large check, anonymously, of course."

"Yes, we know," Steve informed him. "Her parents called us when they got the cashier's check. We had to do a little research, but we were able to back track the funds to the Coalition Committee's bank account. I don't think the committee is going to be pleased about that issue."

Smiling, Von Mumser replied, "That was not a problem. I contributed twice the amount I sent and told the committee treasurer what I wanted to do. Of course I did not say it was because she was a mistake. It was more that I felt sorry for her family. The treasurer had no problem with my request."

"How generous of you. Did it work?" Sal interjected this comment. Changing his attention to Caruso, Von Mumser asked, "Did what work?"

"Easing your conscience. That's what the money was for. So, did it work?"

Giving the question a few seconds thought, Von Mumser replied. "Yes, I believe it did."

Sal did not comment but gave Steve a look that sent a silent thought, "Good luck partner. He's all yours."

"Okay, if Ms. Villareal was a mistake, then all the others were not mistakes. Is that correct?" Steve asked.

"Yes, that is correct," Von Mumser replied.

"Err, Richard...," Pugh began but was cut off by his client.

"No, John, I know what you are going to say. But I said I was going to cooperate and answer all the questions that I could. And that is what I intend to do. After all, I am a man of my word." If he noticed the eye contact occurring among the others in the room, he gave no indication.

"So," Steve stated resuming the questioning, "If the men were not mistakes, what role did they have in your cause?"

"They were volunteers to serve as a focal point in the erroneous thought process of our illustrious judicial system," Von Mumser stated.

"Really?" Stella asked as she joined the questioning. "Mr. Von Mumser why don't you just explain your motive and what it was you envisioned would result from the deaths of your volunteers?"

Von Mumser seemed somewhat amiss that no one there seemed to know what his actions, and the resulting message, were intended to prove. He was disappointed that he had to provide all the information that all of their investigations had missed. Sighing deeply, he knew that if America was ever going to truly understand the gross injustice to the citizens of DC, it was up to him to provide the explanation.

He explained that the Von Mumser family had been in America longer than the birth of this country. His family fought in the American Revolution and every battle since that one in which this nation was involved. His family has lived on the land that is now Washington since arriving in this country. No Von Mumser ever desired to live anywhere else. His family is so entwined in all things Washington that one of his ancestors was part of the original land survey team commissioned by George Washington to lay out the boundaries for the new nation's capitol.

He went on to explain that the problem of obtaining statehood for DC started with the founding fathers and the original thirteen colonies. After centuries and all his family's efforts, he realized that DC would never likely have statehood. He said it was a travesty that those people born in or living in the capitol of the greatest country on earth could not claim statehood. Something gifted, even in mass, to thousands of people not even born here. Often to those who began their life here as illegal immigrants. All the while, those born here in DC, who have lived and died here, are denied that simple American status. He went on to explain that the only form of equality that he could see was to take statehood from those that had it as long as he could not have it. "Thus, I sought out the volunteers to help me send that message," he concluded.

Listening to Von Mumser Stella recognized the man had gone beyond passionate straight into zealot. If he was not redirected to the details they needed, this interrogation would become endless and rhetorical. "Okay, I believe that I can see how you might rationalize this process. But we would like to better understand the selection and screening process for the volunteers."

Von Mumser actually smiled as he began. He told her that it was more qualifications than selections. His expression sobered as he recounted the process. He stated that the more he thought about his particular situation of being a native born Washingtonian, an American without statehood, the more he knew he needed to seek out his counterparts who had statehood. To his way of thinking, it is, and has been, the narrow mindedness of all the state ratifying officials and Congressional members that have kept the District from its' American right to statehood.

That was when he realized that almost without exception; the state ratifying members were white males. For the original thirteen colonies, there were only white males. And it was these same men who began the process of denying statehood to the District. Therefore, he was going to concentrate his strategy against those states and the white male population.

The path of his crusade was quite simple: Begin with the first state and progress to the thirteenth. If his message was not understood at that point, he would consider continuing on to the remaining states. It was in deciding how to begin that he settled on the date that each state was signed into the union. When determining who would best serve his purposes, he decided that it would have to someone with the same qualifications as himself. Therefore he needed white males, who were born and lived in their respective state capitols. Men born in other states did not qualify. It was easy locating these individuals. "People volunteered all sorts of personal information when meeting me in public places," he told them.

"Very interesting," Sal stated. "I see how you came up with your plan. What I want to know is why you selected state capitol buildings as the background for your action. None of these buildings existed at the time of the statehood signings."

Looking at Sal, Von Mumser stated, "I am disappointed in you. Justice is what I was after. Justice. Can't you see that these buildings are symbols of justice?"

During the silence that followed, Maris Ayin sat forward in her chair and spoke. "Mr. Von Mumser, if I may, I have a question."

Looking in the direction of the CDC superintendent, he smiled and replied, "Certainly. I hope I have the answer."

"Through our testing we learned that you used an enhanced version of the chemical warfare agent Phosgene Oxime," Maris stated. "If the manufacture of the original chemical was terminated, and supposedly destroyed by the military, what made you continue working with the deadly toxin?"

"I guess I saw potential in the chemical that the military did not see," he told her. "As you know, its' original intent was to be used as a warfare agent during the cold war. But it never got tested or used. Then the tests were discontinued and the remaining chemical was to be disposed of.

In this case that meant placing it in a metal container and burying it somewhere on the grounds at Aberdeen Proving Grounds. I don't know the exact location where it was buried. I was the Officer-in-Charge of the disposal preparation. About ninety percent of the chemical was buried. I kept ten percent for private research. This is how I was able to enhance the properties from the original state."

"What changes did you make?" Maris asked. "Please, for the record, describe the original intended method of use and how you altered the effects. In plain language please, so everyone can understand."

"Certainly," he told Maris. "It was mostly creative. The original formula gave off vapors and was slow acting. Based on the lab tests I participated in, the chemical when introduced into the body could take from two days up to ten days to end a life. That's ten days of a slow shutdown of someone's internal organs. I believed that the amount of time a person had to suffer was excessive and needed to be greatly shortened.

Through my private experiments I was able to reduce the termination time to thirty minutes to two hours. Plus, the shutdown process was less painful than the original version. The first version attacked the lungs first. My version had lung failure as a final phase. Also, initially, a person needed extensive exposure to the chemical to ensue absorption. My version was developed to ensure immediate absorption upon contact. I was also able to eliminate any vapors. The chemical quickly evaporates when exposed to the air. That was why I had my jacket pockets lined with plastic. To keep them airtight."

"I understand the purpose of the lined pockets," Maris stated. "We found your antidote, which obviously served as your personal protection. But, how were you able to ensure that only those you selected were infected? I understand how you used the business cards as the method of infection. But how did you ensure that no one else got infected from any residue left in your pockets?"

"It wasn't that difficult," he told her. "The plastic linings are secured with Velcro. When I returned to my hotel room, or my home, I would remove the linings and clean them with an antiseptic swab. After the linings were dry, I disposed of them. Actually, you know, the chemicals used at a dry cleaners can cause more skin and lung damage than any residual elements that might have remained on my jackets. I determined, and ensured, that no innocent person would be infected by accident."

"And those men whose lives you took just because they were born in their state's capitol were not innocent?" Steve asked in a strained tone.

"No, they were not innocent," Von Mumser responded. "The people of Washington, DC are innocent. Those men will be remembered as a testament to the value of statehood for all the people of America. It can't be the United States of America AND the District of Columbia anymore. It must just be the United States of America, period. Surely Congress must be aware of their error in thinking by now."

Stella looked at her team members and Maris. No one had any more questions at this point. She told the federal security officer that he could escort Mr. Von Mumser to the holding area until he was transported to a federal facility. She thanked Von Mumser for being so informative and told Mrs. Von Mumser that she would tell the judge about her husband's cooperation. Stella did not know if it would help in his case, but she would let the authorities know. Sandra Von Mumser thanked Stella and left the room with John Pugh.

Out in the hallway Jack Yu and Julius Walsh watched in amazement as Richard Von Mumser was led away in handcuffs. Then Mrs. Von Mumser came out into the hallway. Jack Yu stood up to greet her. When Sandra saw Jack, she embraced him and with a chocked voice told him, "Oh, Jack, I am so sorry. I know how much he means to you. I am so sorry all this had to even happen." Pulling back she took Jack's surprised looking face in her hands. "Please, don't hate him. He really meant to do good things." Backing away from Jack she added, "Say a prayer for him Jack. He will need it." Sandra turned, allowed John Pugh to take her elbow and lead her down the corridor.

Turning back to look at Julius, who was standing a few feet away, Jack confessed how crushed he was at the resulting situation. In a rare moment of confidentiality Jack told Julius how much he has always idolized Von Mumser, even considered him a role model. He related how Von Mumser had saved his father's life during Desert Storm and that he must ensure that his father never learned of this. His father, he explained, lives in a nursing home and suffers from Alzheimer's, and in a lucid moment, this information would devastate him. Then, realizing what he had said, he told Julius that he would appreciate not reading about this personal information in any of Walsh's articles about Von Mumser. Julius promised not to reveal this latest conversation, but could not promise not to mention Jack and what is already public knowledge. Jack looked at Julius, nodded his head in understanding, then extended his hand and shook hands with the reporter. "See you around the neighborhood," Julius told him as he picked up his camera and walked down the corridor to see if he could speak with Von Mumser.

As Jack bent to retrieve his overcoat and leave the building, he stopped. Stella was standing in the doorway to the interrogation room. Jack had no idea how long she had been standing there or how much she had overheard. But, by the look on her face, she had been standing there for awhile. As he started to walk past her, she put her hand on his arm to stop him. "If that offer is still there, I would like that cup of coffee now." He looked at her for a few seconds, gave one nod of his head, then a slight smile. "Sure, the offer is still there and that sounds good to me."

Chapter XXXI

May 24, 2015
DC Daily Newspaper Brief
Washington DC

HEADLINE: Chairman for Life
Byline: Julius Walsh

After much deliberation, Federal Judge Pinchanski, agreed to a no-contest plea from Richard Von Mumser, former Chairman of the Coalition Committee for DC Statehood. This action puts a halt to the partitions from various states for trial rights.

Based on Mr. Von Mumser's full cooperation with the authorities, he has received twenty-two consecutive life sentences, without parole, and has been placed in a maximum federal facility.

Family members of the victims are still filing suits against both the Von Mumser family estate and the Coalition Committee.
(See Chairman on page A-4)

Epilogue

June 9, 2015
Mayor's Conference Area
Washington, DC

Today was definitely the absolute best day of his life. Not only was this his birthday, officially a teenager now. But, thirteen year old Brandon Cohen was about to be the very center of national attention. Boy was this ever going to change his Nerd status.

Since the request came last week for his presence at an award ceremony, he has been a local celebrity. He was not able to walk from one class to the next without being stopped by dozens of students. Many of them never gave Brandon the time of day before. But now, they looked at him with respect. Some of the girls even asked him out for after school snacks at the local mall. The kids started calling him Young Sherlock Holmes. Brandon literally blossomed from the attention.

Harvey was elated with happiness and pride. He was sure that this adventure was exactly what Brandon needed to let him know that smarts can be a good thing. Jodie wasn't to be left out of all the excitement either. She was drawing her own form of notoriety as "Sherlock's Sister". Always proud of her brother, she was even more gratified with the attention he was receiving.

The award ceremony was scheduled for ten a.m. in the Washington, DC Mayor's conference area. Brandon was accompanied by his father and his sister. Brandon was to be presented with an Outstanding Citizen Medal from the District of Columbia. The attendee list was very impressive, even by local political standards. The medal was to be presented by the Mayor of DC and the Director of the FBI.

THE COALITION

The Senators and Governors from Delaware, Pennsylvania, New Jersey, Georgia, Connecticut, Massachusetts, and Maryland would be present. The room also held family members of the victims. Also invited were Stella Vega, Sal Caruso, and Steve Woods. Maris Ayin, also in attendance, was honored to have her son, Joseph, with her.

The Editor of the DC Daily assigned this event to Julius Walsh. Wellen knew that Walsh was going to write a book about this episode in DC legacy and wanted to ensure that Walsh's position as a DC Daily reporter got credit for such exclusive coverage. Seemed Julius was going to have his "moment in history" story after all, just not with the outcome he had anticipated.

The icing on the cake for Brandon was the invitation from Bubba Meisah to be a guest on his morning talk show the day after the award ceremony. Without hesitation, and after consulting with his father, he accepted the invitation. Yes, life surely had a good side.

All the attendees watched with collective enthusiasm as Mayor Jackson, flanked by the FBI Director and the Senate Majority Leader presented the District of Columbia's Outstanding Citizen Medal to Brandon Cohen. Brandon, flanked by his father and his sister, turned a beatific face to the group of reporters and flashing cameras.

Printed in the United States
50738LVS00002B/535-621